Carol,
Always Keep Romance in your life;
Jeanne Winters

SOUTHERN EXPOSURE

SOUTHERN DESIRES SERIES

Book Two

by
Jeannette Winters

Author Contact

website:
JeannetteWinters.com

email:
authorjeannettewinters@gmail.com

Facebook:
Author Jeannette Winters

Twitter:
JWintersAuthor

Mark Collins dedicates his life to serve and protect in the Navy. He excels at what he does but at the cost of being emotionally detached.

Hannah Entwistle left her small hometown to follow her dreams. Just when they are within reach, she had to return to care for her father.

Torn between honoring a promise to restore the family homestead and wanting to follow her heart, Hannah finds herself in a place she never wanted to be: lost and alone in Savannah.

Mark wasn't expecting complications when he chose this job on the side, but her southern charm storms his defenses. When her life is threatened, will duty trump love?

Copyright

Dedication

This book is dedicated to John Turchetta who is an inspiration and challenged me to write this series with the flavor of intrigue. Through your knowledge and insight, you brought Mark Collins to life. This book would not be the same without you.

Also dedicated to Denise Bailey. Your messages and cards filled with wisdom will be treasured always as you encourage me to keep it real. Thank you!

I am also supported by a team of beta readers who aren't afraid to tell me the truth. Thank you for that!

Karen Lawson, Janet Hitchcock, E.L. King and Marion Arche, my editors you are all amazing!

To my readers who brings joy into my life with each and every message. Always make time for romance

CHAPTER ONE

*T*OO *DAMN QUIET* Mark Collins thought, sitting in one of the many white rocking chairs on the porch. He'd always been more of a hammock-with-a-cold-beer kind of guy, but he'd take what he could get at the moment. Any time he had a break from his job or training for the Navy Special Forces, he tried to keep it low-key, but this was more than he could take. Sitting still was a requirement, not something he'd ever choose to do to pass the time.

It was hot as hell, but Savannah, Georgia in mid-July gave hot a whole new definition. Mark didn't need a thermometer to tell it was close to one hundred degrees, and the humidity was through the roof. *I'd love a beer, but heck, I'd settle for lemonade right now.*

Savannah sounded like a great place to spend a month or two while between assignments, but if the owner didn't arrive soon, she was going to find herself looking for another handyman. Mark was known for a lot of things, but patience wasn't one of them.

His phone rang. He wasn't hoping there was an

emergency, but if this wasn't the owner saying she was five minutes away, then he'd just as soon be called away to a desert somewhere doing something . . . anything. Looking at the caller ID, he wasn't sure if he was relieved or not. It was his sister, Casey, who he'd reluctantly left in the hands of her fiancé, Derrick Nash. He'd wanted to stay and watch over her, but she'd made it clear that he'd be intruding in their lives. *But an intrusion is better than a funeral.*

Georgia wasn't all that far from Texas, but until the men his sister had exposed for negligence were behind bars, he wasn't going to let his guard down. Thankfully Derrick was of the same opinion.

"Hi, Mark. I'm checking to see if you made it to Savannah."

You're checking on me? Something's not right. "Talk to me, Casey." There was a brief pause, and he thought he was going to leap through the phone to get her to speak. If she was in trouble, he would've heard from his men long before Casey called him. "What's wrong?"

He knew her well. They stayed in contact as often as was humanly possible, given his job. But with their parents still overseas, Mark had more reason than ever to keep a constant, watchful eye on his baby sister. *Not that she appreciates all the extra attention, but her irritation isn't going to stop me from protecting her.* If there was even the slightest hint of a single, negative repercussion heading her way, he and his men would be back on the ranch in a heartbeat.

"Nothing is wrong," she sighed heavily. "Derrick and I are getting married, and I want to talk to you about it."

He wanted to pound his head against the wooden rail in front of him. *Your life could be at risk with a criminal investigation underway on your former boss, and you call to talk about a wedding? Damn, I'll never understand women. Never.* "Wouldn't you rather call Mom or one of your friends back home? Or how about your new friend, Sissie? I know she'd love to hear all about it." *I'm not sure Sissie can listen when she talks so damn much. I'm still hoping her cousin Hannah isn't as wild and loud as she is.*

"I'm not calling to discuss flowers and dresses. Do you think I've lost my mind? I mean, I do owe you payback from the last time I saw you, but torturing you with color choices and bridesmaid dresses might be too much." Casey laughed.

"Okay, then what's going on? Getting cold feet?"

"Cold feet, no. But panicking, yes. Derrick and I hadn't set a date when you left. Now we have, and we're getting married in two weeks."

"What's the rush?"

"We want something small here on the ranch. Waiting won't change anything because getting you all home at the same time is nearly impossible. Besides, I want to get married while Dad is still able to walk me down the aisle."

He heard the sadness in Casey's voice. Their father had ALS, and it was only a matter of time before he lost the ability to move around. The last time he'd spoken to his mother, she'd told him their father's left leg was getting weak, and he'd fallen a few times. When Mark had tried to get them to come home, they'd refused.

Dad, you're one of the strongest, selfless, and most stubborn men I know. This world would be a better place if people could even be half the man you are.

"Your mother and I will come home when we can no longer help here," his father had said in his end-of-discussion voice. *Damn proud man. Damn good man.* Casey's wedding was just the thing to bring them back to the States. *If only he realized that his daughter needed him more than strangers halfway across the world. I could tell him she's dealing with a federal investigation and shouldn't face this alone. But he would only say what he said before, "That's what she has brothers for." I can protect her, but what she needs is you, Dad, to be home where you can get the medical attention you need. I respect your decisions as you have always respected mine, but it doesn't mean I agree with you.*

"It makes sense to me."

"So I'll send you all the information. I hope you're still stateside then. It'll mean the world to me to have you there. You can even bring a date."

Bring a date? Where the hell did that come from? I hope she's not expecting me to follow in her footsteps. I'm happy for her and all, but there is no way I'm bringing a date. Never have before, and I'm not about to start now. Damn, she'll be lucky if I make it there.

Mark was thirty-eight, and he'd never brought anyone home to meet the family. It'd only open up questions he couldn't nor wouldn't answer. One would think his mother would be the one pressuring him about starting a family, but it blew his mind that it was his father playing the thousand-questions game. "When are you ever going to settle down and get married? The Navy won't keep you warm at night." *Good ole Dad. I'm sure you're going to be pushing even harder at Casey's wedding. Just one more thing to look forward to.*

"You know I'll be there if I can." Mark never made promises. They'd only be broken. He'd do his best. If he wasn't on assignment, then he'd be there.

"Promise me, Mark." Her tone was pleading, but he was immune to such tactics. "This is my wedding we're talking about. Your *only* sister's big day. I want you there. I need you there."

Nothing she could say would change anything. It wasn't that he didn't love his family, because he did. If they were in trouble, he would do everything in his power to protect them much like he had recently done for Casey.

But he knew himself. His life was the Navy. He fought for his parents' consent to join at age seventeen. The day after he graduated high school he was on the bus heading to basic training. That was why he chose to live an unattached lifestyle with no one waiting for him to come home. Mark had a team that counted on him. They never let him down, and he wasn't about to do it to them. *No matter how much I love you, sis, I can only promise to be there if I can. Any more than that would be a lie.*

She knew the choices he made were always centered on his call to duty. Normally Casey didn't pressure him like this.

"What's really going on? Is everything okay with you and Derrick?" *If he's not treating you right, let me know. I'll be there in three hours to correct it, end it, whatever needs to be done. Just say it and it will be done.*

"I love Derrick. He's amazing. Of course, sometimes I think you overdid drilling into his head about protecting me. I know the investigation of JT and the death of Derrick's wife and daughter is still open, but I've been taking care of myself for years. I don't need a babysitter."

Excellent, Derrick. That's what I like to hear. Keep my sister safe. "Do you want my men back at the ranch? Say the word and I'll make a call."

"No!"

Mark laughed. He knew it was an empty threat, but Casey didn't, and that was all that mattered. He'd spoken to Derrick in depth, and together they'd agreed she was safe on the ranch. Casey was in good hands with his soon-to-be brother-in-law. *Still, I can't believe my baby sister is getting married. Better her than me.*

"So did you talk to Mom and Dad?"

"Yes, and they're flying back early next week so Mom can help me pull things together. It's going to be small, but I want her here, want her involved."

Perfect. "Did you call your favorite brother and let

him know?" Mark loved teasing Casey.

"I love you both equally," she stated seriously as she always did. "But yes, I called Kevin."

Even though she said she loved them equally, Mark had acted as the protector so often that they had butted heads growing up. Kevin never complained as he said it took the heat off him. Mark was close to his brother but knew Kevin could handle himself. It was Casey he worried about then, and still did now. *Letting go of that isn't going to be easy. I hope Derrick is up to the challenge, because I have no problem stepping in if I think I'm needed.*

"So, I'm last on your list?" He could picture her face turning red. Pushing her buttons was easy. He never teased anyone else, but his kid sister was fair game.

"Mark Collins, you drive me crazy," Casey said right before laughing. "I tell you what, you can call me last when you invite me to *your* wedding one day."

You're going to be waiting a long time for a call I'm never going to make. "Okay, Casey, you have a deal."

Mark laughed because he knew it was a deal he would never need to worry about. There was no room in his life for that type of connection. He had his family to think about: his parents, Casey, Kevin, and the men on his team who were as much family as his siblings were. It wasn't that he didn't enjoy the company of a woman, but he didn't need the complication of commitment that came along with them. *Sorry, Mom, but I'll leave it to Casey and Kevin to provide the grandkids you have been waiting for.*

Casey's voice became serious. "I want you there, Mark. You never know when this could be the last time we're all together. If I learned anything from Derrick, it's to not waste precious time. No one is guaranteed tomorrow, and you and Kevin should know that. You both put yourselves in the line of fire and we never know when . . ."

Death was something he faced but refused to think about. It would only make him less effective, and he couldn't afford that. That kind of distraction would not only risk his life, but the men he led as well.

"I'll be there if I can." *I hear her loud and clear, and she's right. We need to be there as a family. If not for her, then for Mom and Dad.*

"Good. I'll see you in a couple weeks, Mark," Casey stated before she disconnected the call.

Sure. Now let's hope nothing goes wrong, and I don't get pulled overseas. I'm never worried about making a decision, but who to let down is one I'd rather not make. Love you, sis, but you know which one I'd have to choose. Duty first. Most people would cave to the pressure, but not him. Maybe he should've let her believe he would be there no matter what, but he couldn't bring himself to mislead her. His duty to his country and his men always came first. *She knows that, even if it's hard to accept.*

The last thing he wanted to think about was breaking his kid sister's heart. Keeping busy was a great way to avoid that, however, his project in Savannah wasn't moving very fast. *Or at all for that matter.*

He looked at his watch. Thirteen hundred hours. Hannah was already an hour late. If she didn't arrive soon, he was going to get right back into his Jeep Cherokee and find himself another short-term project. *People in need are easy to come by, unfortunately.*

Mark hadn't actually spoken to Hannah, the owner. All communication had been through text messages. Both she and her cousin, Sissie, had made it clear she was in desperate need of the help. He was here, ready and able.

Okay. Enough of this shit. Getting off the chair, Mark stood and stretched. He walked up and down the length of the porch. He could see why she requested his help. The fresh flower baskets hanging all around and colorful cushions on the chairs made the place look nice, but they were a poor cover-up for the chipping paint on the rails. And the planks on the deck had protruding nails. *It has a woman's touch, but damn this place needs a man's hand, or it's going to fall apart around her.*

Mark didn't need her permission to bang in nails; they were raised so high they would be considered a trip hazard. *I'll fix these then I'm out.*

Leaving the shade of the porch, he walked to his Jeep, pulled off his already drenched T-shirt and threw it inside on the driver's seat. *I've been in worse situations. Much worse.* There were places he'd seen that'd make hell seem like a walk in the park. Despite the oppressive heat, Savannah was a beautiful city. He could understand why people would want to live there and raise a family.

Mark walked to the back of his beat-up Jeep, lifted the hatch, opened the cooler, and pulled out a cold bottle of water. Drinking half, he poured the remainder over his head. When he wasn't on duty, he let his hair and beard grow civilian to look less obvious and avoid questions he wasn't going to answer. *At least, not honestly.* Lying was a job requirement. No one truly knew where he was or what he did. Not even those closest to him, a fact he was simply used to after years in the Navy Special Forces.

As he faced the house, he could picture what it must've looked like when it was well maintained. The massive white Georgian Colonial must have been a single family home. It was two-stories tall, each level with a huge porch held up by tall wooden columns, and made for entertaining. Now you'd build a deck instead. Back home they had nothing compared to this fine piece of architecture. *Of course in Buffalo, the Snowbelt from hell, there's a good part of the year no one in his right mind stands outside on a porch.* The snow back home appealed to him less the more time he spent in hot deserts over-seas. It wasn't that his body had adapted to the heat; he just hated the cold more.

Hannah had said the house had been converted to four apartments, one of them hers. Whoever had taken on that renovation must've invested a lot of time and money. Renovating old homes sometimes had a domino effect. *Fix one thing and watch the rest fall apart.* It had lost its luster and looked neglected. *Give me a few months and I could work some magic here.* Home remolding wasn't his job; it was a hobby, a distraction. There were times he needed the work more than the homeowner needed him. *Thankfully this wasn't one of those times.*

Their last deployment had been in and out without issue or casualty. Just the way they liked it. But sometimes he relished and welcomed the simplicity of building, painting, or whatever the job required of him. Otherwise he might have suffered terribly from the night terrors associated with war. He knew the importance of keeping so busy he had no time to think. Work so hard you pass out, too tired to dream.

He reminded himself that all he'd seen so far was the outside of the apartment house. None of what he saw was on the to-do list Hannah had texted him. *If she considers this in good shape, I can only imagine what the rest of the place looks like.*

Mark grabbed his tool belt and headed for the porch. Even though she didn't feel the need to show up on time, he didn't plan on sitting there doing nothing all afternoon. Not when there were so many repairs staring him in the face, waiting to be done. *I've come all this way. Might as well accomplish something.*

The wood hadn't rotted away, and he was able to bang in the loose nails and reinforce the railing that was about to topple over. As he looked over his handy work, he knew it was only a start to what looked like a major renovation. *Maybe I should call for reinforcements on this assignment.*

The first couple times he went on the road he'd traveled light, sometimes only with a change of clothes. He honestly hadn't been looking for work back then, just a diversion. But over the last few years, he'd sought out people who needed a helping hand. He never had to look far, as times were tough and many had their hands out. That's when he learned to travel prepared for almost anything. Not only did he have most tools to handle basic repairs, but also his duffle bag packed and ready in case he got the call. Usually, he made it back to the base first, but over the past year that hadn't always been possible. Most assignments had been overseas, but trouble was now hitting closer to home than anyone wanted to admit. He and his team needed to be ready at a moment's notice. On more than one occasion he'd had no choice but to leave a homeowner high and dry in the middle of a remodel without any explanation. He'd received many irate text messages from them without being able to defend his actions. *All par for the course.*

He wasn't worried about Hannah being pissed at him. *Hell, she can't even remember how to tell time, never mind noticing if I disappear.*

As he put his tools back in the Jeep, a yellow Volkswagen convertible pulled up beside him with a country love song blaring. He didn't need to look to know the driver was young. There was no way this was Hannah. She was Sissie's cousin and probably around her age.

A woman wearing a light blue and white polka-dotted vintage dress got out of the car and walked over to him. The dress hugged her torso—*and perfect full breasts*—like a glove. It wasn't the heat of the day getting him hot at the moment. He normally had more couth than to stare, but damn, he couldn't bring himself to look away. Even the flared skirt, leaving her hips to his imagination, enticed him. It hadn't been that long since he'd had a woman, but his body was reacting like it had been years.

His eyes finally made their way back to her face. *Stunning.* Golden-blonde long, loose curls hung sweetly, enhancing her already young, innocent look. As his eyes met her deep green eyes, he was drawn to her even more. *Beautiful, but dangerous as hell.*

"Excuse me, sir, can I help you with something?"

She even had the voice of an angel. Whoever this woman was, she needed to go before he forgot he was a gentleman, never mind here to do a job.

"Nope. I'm here to work, and you're definitely not dressed to assist." *Hinder? Yes. Help? No.* With her close by, he wasn't sure he'd be able to hit a nail on the head. His eyes roamed her body from head to toe. Maybe his last few deployments were longer than most, but there was nothing he didn't find appealing about her.

If he thought he was making her uncomfortable, he was mistaken. Those inquisitive eyes of hers roamed up and down his body as though he was a prized bull. *Keep looking at me like that, young lady, and we're going to have an issue. A sweet, delicious issue.*

"Laaawdy. Sissie just became my favorite cousin." Until then he hadn't noticed her southern accent.

Mark had been referred to this job by Sissie. But she was much older than this young thing. She looked to be in her early twenties, which freaked him out with the thoughts running through his mind. It had to be her mother he was here to meet, not her. *Please, not her.*

"I think I'm here to meet your mother," Mark said as he pulled a clean T-shirt out of his bag and pulled it over his head. She never took her eyes off him. *Don't tempt me to pull you into my arms and test how sweet and innocent you really are. Damn. I don't know if I want her sweet or hot and wild. Either way, she's one person I need to keep at a distance.*

"Well, sorry to inform you, but you're twenty-eight years too late." He arched a brow, and she continued. "My mother died shortly after giving birth to me."

Oh hell. "What about your father?"

"He passed away last year."

Oh double hell. Foot in the mouth issue, Collins? That's not usually a problem you suffer from. Fucking snap out of it.

Although she was trying to cover up the pain and extend her southern warm welcome, it was shining through her eyes. Mark watched her closely. Reading people was part of his job. What was it she wasn't saying? The hurt seemed to include more than just losing both her parents, although that must have been hard enough. Something she didn't want anyone to see. That only made him more curious. When things seemed odd, he made it his mission to find the answer. Nothing was as simple as it seemed to be, and that's exactly what he thought looking at her.

Mark reminded himself he was here for one reason only: to handle household repairs. Anything beyond that was off limits. And with how she looked at him, he knew it was already going to be difficult.

"I'm working for you? You're Hannah?" he asked even though he knew the answer. He just didn't like it.

"In the flesh and blood," she replied sweetly, with a teasing roll of her shoulders.

Damn. I should've left when I had the chance. As soon as she was late, that Jeep should've headed back to Buffalo. She would only be one thing—a complication. And I never have and never will allow any of those in my life. Don't need them. The day Sissie told him about her cousin she'd played it off that Hannah was frail and older. It'd been a long time since anyone had been able to pull one on him. He had to give it to her. She was good. Mark had two options: ignore the lovely in front of him and do the job, or walk away and let her find someone more suitable.

He reached out a hand and said, "I'm Mark Collins, your contractor for the next month or so."

She placed her delicate hand in his. It was cool and soft against his rough one. "Welcome, I'm Hannah Entwistle, the lucky person who has inherited this monstrosity of a home, and it looks like you're the lucky man who'll make it shine again."

Shine? How about we strive for sturdy? "Let's see what we're working with before you get your hopes up." Mark already knew he wasn't the right person for this job. If the exterior was any indication of what the interior looked like, this was going to need a crew, not one handyman, to whip it back into shape. He couldn't even guarantee how long he was going to be on the job.

"Why don't you come on in, and I'll show you where you can put your things while you're here."

Mark thought she'd apologize for keeping him waiting so long out in the heat, but not one word. Could she really be that clueless? He'd been waiting almost two hours for her. He was so punctual that it drove people crazy. He didn't expect everyone to feel the same as him, but this was ridiculous. "Do you know what time it is?"

He stood there amazed at how carefree she was as she answered. "Nope, but I know it's Saturday. A stress-free day."

Glad one of us isn't stressed.

"You know I lost an entire day's work already."

"And you're going to lose another one tomorrow. We don't work on weekends. Things around here are much more relaxed."

And there is the answer why the house looks like it does. He wasn't looking forward to sitting around for a second day. All he needed was to see what had to be fixed, and he'd make his own schedule, weekends included.

Hannah turned and headed to the house.

"Where are we going?" Mark asked, still standing by his Jeep.

She turned back and said, "My apartment. I have a guest room ready for you."

There is no way she's inviting a perfect stranger into her house. She should check my ID, confirm that I am who I say I am. If this was Casey, I'd have— Who was he fooling? Casey had become stubborn. When she was young, she'd listen to his voice of reason. Not any longer. *Maybe Derrick will have better luck.*

He didn't know why his temper was soaring, but he couldn't hold his tongue any longer.

"How naïve are you?" His tone was harsh. "You met me less than five minutes ago, and you're inviting me into your home? Not only that, you're actually considering letting me stay in your apartment?" She knew nothing about him except that her cousin Sissie sent him. "I could be anyone with less-than-honorable intentions just waiting for the opportunity to get you alone so I could—"

"Are you?" Her voice was calm and soft.

"Am I what?" Mark snapped at her.

"A creep or a pervert waiting to hurt me?" she asked with her hands on her hips. There was no hint she was joking, but he was tempted to laugh. What person would actually admit it? *You are that naïve.*

"No."

"Well, then what is the problem?"

There was no making her see any differently at this

point. *Oh, you sweet girl. You truly have no clue, do you? Looks like there is a lot more work to be done here than just repairing an old rundown house.* "None I guess."

He reached in the Jeep, grabbed his duffle bag, and went to stand by her on the porch. *You're lucky I took an oath to serve and protect.*

HANNAH'S HEART WAS pounding even though she refused to let it show. Sissie hadn't said what Mark looked like. If anything she played it off like he was an older retired gentleman who did this work for fun. *Not even close, Sissie. Unless she's recently become blind, which I don't think happened, then she's up to something.*

Mark seemed to want to hide his good looks under a mass of unruly hair and a beard that needed a trim. But when she pulled up and found him shirtless, she almost melted. Every muscle was cut and defined, begging her to trace them with her fingers.

Slow down, girl. This man is not here to get ogled. He's here for work. Hannah needed to stay focused. There was so much work to be done, and she had limited funds. If it wasn't for the fact that Mark was willing to work for peanuts, she knew it was only a matter of time before this old house began falling down around her. *Here to work, no distracting him.* That didn't mean she wasn't going to enjoy the view as he worked.

She was smiling as she held the front door open and went into the main hallway. "There are four apartments as I mentioned before. Each apartment is set up similar to mine with two bedrooms, living room, full bath, but their kitchens are smaller than mine. Since I have the side with the original kitchen, we left it large. I guess my father thought I would want to cook for an army one day because it is way too big for just me. I don't think I mentioned that my father did all the renovations himself. The original house had eight large bedrooms upstairs with two full bathrooms. You'll see that he moved two bedrooms downstairs and added kitchens in each apartment, but he wasn't able to complete all the work, so you'll have your work cut out for you." She looked him over. *He looks like he could handle just about anything thrown at him.* "I have one rented upstairs on the left to the perfect tenant. I never see or hear him. He even slips the cash under my door each month on time."

"That doesn't strike you as odd?" Mark asked as he stared up the staircase.

Not when he pays me. "He minds his business, and I do the same." She was already struggling financially and couldn't afford to question every little thing. If she had her way, she'd fill the place with people just like him. "The top right is vacant, but I have someone looking at it the end of next week. I've let people look before, but there is still work to be done in there before anyone will want to move in. If there's anything you can do before they come and take a look, it might be a great help in getting it rented." *Rent means money, and money means I won't lose this place. The one problem is it's going to take money to get it up to par, and that is one thing I don't have right now. How did I ever get in this bind?*

She knew the answer, but there had never really been a choice. And she would do it again. Her father's medical expenses had cleared out every cent he'd had as well as hers. She didn't regret any of it. He'd been a wonderful, loving, supportive father and she'd do it all over again if it meant having more time with him. But now she was left without a degree and faced paying her student loans on a very limited income. If it weren't for her promise to her father, she'd have left this place a year ago. Instead she was here in limbo, unable to let go of the past and unable to move forward. She had to make this place work. Then she could take some time to think about what she wanted. It'd been so long since she'd given that a serious thought, but she wasn't ready to let go, to say goodbye.

Leaving this house and moving to a much smaller place was a logical solution. If she had stayed in college, she'd be working as a vet somewhere instead of part-time waitressing at Al's Diner. After her father passed away, she'd thought about going back to college, picking up where she'd left off. But the truth was, she didn't have it in her then. She was out of the studying groove and the courses she'd be required to take were mentally taxing. The longer she went without returning, the harder it became. Now she was too far in debt to even consider going back to school. This place was all she had to fall back on.

I hate to admit it, but you're my last chance to make

this work so I can get out of here. Sissie sent you here for a reason. It better be to work, Mark, or you're going to find yourself out of here in a flash.

"I can't make a promise until I see what shape it's in."

She was glad he didn't promise her the moon as others had. *They'd say they wanted to help me with the house, but in fact, it wasn't the house they were interested in. I might be alone, but I'm not that type of girl.*

She'd never been a typical southern flirt. She was shy and reserved. Her only boyfriend had been in her first year of college. She knew he wasn't the one for a long term relationship. So when he said he wanted to just be friends, she'd been in total agreement.

"The bottom left is vacant as well. I live in this one on the right." She pointed to her closed door.

He stood so quiet and still as she spoke that she found it unnerving. She could see in his eyes he was in deep thought. Was he already regretting taking on the job? She couldn't blame him. The pay was horrible and the work hard. Not something anyone with a brain would find appealing. Dwelling on what she couldn't change was only going to stress her. Forcing herself to ignore his strange behavior, she began providing him with more details.

"I don't know what tools you brought with you, but there's a doorway to the backyard behind the staircase. There's a shed outside with additional tools. I've no idea what good they'll be or if they're what you'll need to do the job, but you can use any you need. They haven't been touched since . . . well not in a few years."

She tried not to think of those last few years her dad had been alive. When things became too much for him to be on his own, she did what any daughter would do: put her life on hold. She left college with three years to complete so she could be home by his side. One year became two and then time quickly slipped away, just as her father had. Where had the time gone? One minute she was a child sliding down the long oak banisters from top to bottom and the next she was off to college in Rhode Island and starting a life of her own. *Or so I thought. Now I'm back to square one and stuck in a house filled with memories. It's almost too much to bear.*

She needed to snap out of it. *There's no future in yesterday.* "Let me put my purse in my room, then I'll show you where you can put your bag." Hannah opened the door to her apartment and went inside.

Mark stood just outside the door as though it wasn't open. "I noticed you didn't unlock the front door. You don't lock the door to your apartment either?"

She shrugged. "The deadbolt lock on the apartment door broke off on the inside about a year ago. It's on your list to fix."

"A year ago? You're living in this house with some guy you don't know anything about upstairs, and you don't even have a lock on your door?"

He was shaking his head in disbelief. She didn't see what the issue was. This was her family home. She didn't know where he came from and what the people were like there, but in all the years she'd lived here, not even something as small as a paper clip had gone missing. The good people of Savannah took care of each other. They loved and supported each other; they might borrow something but, to her knowledge, never stole anything. *Such was the quandary of southern life. You either loved it and never wanted to leave, or you felt the ties but needed to spread your wings elsewhere. What's wrong with me that even though this is my home town, I still feel like an outsider?*

"You make it seem much worse than it is."

"Make it number one on that list," Mark said sternly.

Boy, he's so uptight. I think he needs a vacation more than he needs to work. "Has anyone ever told you that you worry too much?"

He was staring at her so seriously when he replied, "Every person I meet."

Hannah wasn't going to let his stress become hers. Teasingly she said, "Oh, here I thought you were just being overly protective of me." *Not that I wouldn't appreciate someone to look after me once in a while. I've learned there is only one person I can count on, and that's me.*

When Mark finally entered her apartment she thought he might relax a bit. Instead he dropped his duffle bag on the floor and instantly went into fix-it mode, looking at the door. By his expression, he wasn't too happy with what he found. She may have failed to mention the entire locking mechanism had fallen out on the inside.

"Where's the lock?"

"Some pieces are on the shelf behind you," he went to retrieve them as she continued, "but I threw out some of it too."

Mark picked up the lock then turned back to her. "By some you mean the actual part where the key goes? This is useless."

"Wow. Thanks for clarifying that. I couldn't have figured that out myself." It wasn't like her to be so sarcastic. She was hot and tired, and a lecture from hired help was not going to make it any better. She'd lived there most of her life, and her father had never locked a door. "My father always said 'a lock only keeps a good person from entering. It never stops a criminal.'"

Of course I didn't use that when I went to college. There you had a lock for everything, and if you didn't, it seemed to grow legs and walk.

"How about this one, an ounce of prevention—"

"Okay, I hear you. Monday we'll go into town and get a new lock. Happy?"

"Let's go now." Mark tossed what remained of the lock onto the desk by the door.

"Impossible."

"Why?"

"Because they close at noon on the weekends. So it'll have to wait until Monday." *And the last thing I want right now is another long drive into town. If I take him there now, my phone will be blowing up with questions all weekend about who he is, what he is doing here. And I hate questions. Not everyone asks questions because they care about the answers, and I'm tired of people asking me if I'm okay when they really don't want to hear the truth. Sometimes I just can't bring myself to smile and answer, "Wonderful." Sometimes I want to yell and scream and say life is not fair. But no, I can't do that here. Not unless I want to be the talk of the town. That's what I liked about the big city. People knew boundaries. They didn't care who you were or what you did as long as it didn't affect them. Again, the complexity of southern, small-town living where you both hate it and love it.*

"And that is the only place to shop?"

Hannah put her hands on her hips. "You know, Mr. Collins, you ask a lot of questions, as though you're not a very trusting person. Why is that?"

"Because I don't go through life with rose-colored glasses. Maybe it's time you take yours off."

She was shocked by his gruff, condescending words. It wasn't like she didn't know how cruel life could be. Her life hadn't been an easy one, not that she shared any of it—even with her best friend. Life could be very ugly. If anyone doubted that all they needed to do was turn on the television for a constant reminder. She made a choice every day to get up, put a smile on her face, and be happy. "We can add a pair of glasses to your shopping list on Monday." Hannah put her nose in the air, claiming victory as she brushed past him, but she knew it was far from the truth. *He's not coming here and making me look at the bad. Maybe I need to teach him how to see the bright side of things. And from what I've seen so far, it looks like I'll have my hands full with more than just supervising the repairs the next few months.*

CHAPTER TWO

MARK DIDN'T SLEEP much that night, as usual. After two or three hours he was awake and ready to go. He couldn't remember the last time he was up after sunrise. Even on a day like today when he could've spent a day in bed because he obviously wasn't going to be allowed to get any work done, he couldn't sleep. His internal clock told him it was around three a.m.

There were numerous people he could call right now who were up and pacing the floor just like him. The only time his team wasn't up this damn early was when they were passed out from being drunk the night before. Many nights he was tempted to do the same so he could relax, but he couldn't let his guard down. Mark needed to be ready, be in control, *at all times*. When you're shit-faced drunk as hell, mistakes get made, and people get hurt or worse. He'd seen it happen to others. It wasn't going to happen to him or his men. Not if he could help it.

Before he called it a night last night, he'd taken a look at her apartment. The original wood was still intact.

The only change he could see was to the inner walls where they made what must've been a living room into bedrooms. She hadn't shown him hers, but he assumed it was the one door she refused to open. If it was anything like her, it probably was bright and colorful. *And smelled of honeysuckles.*

There was only one bathroom, and it separated their bedrooms. Hearing Hannah singing in the shower late last night didn't help his sleep any, but he knew where the saying *voice of an angel* came from. It was exotically sensual and soothing to the soul. He'd found himself lying on the bed with his eyes closed, totally relaxed. It was such a bittersweet rarity. No matter how he yearned to hear it again, next time he was going out for a walk.

Actually, a walk now might be a good idea. Mark pulled a flashlight from his bag. This was a good time to check out that shed Hannah had mentioned to him the night before. He had tools but supplies to do the job were another story. There didn't seem to be anything that didn't creak as he opened it or walked on it, but the noise didn't seem to wake Hannah. Many times over the years in the field, being stealthy was what saved his life.

He stopped by the kitchen where she'd shown him the one thing he wasn't going to start this day without. *Coffee.* Grabbing a mug he put it under the dispenser and pressed the button for bold. He liked it strong and black. When he took his first sip, he nearly spat it right back out again; it tasted more like colored water. Downing the hot contents he rinsed the cup and put it back in the cupboard. There was a sink full of dishes waiting to be washed, but that didn't matter to him. Mark had been alone so long that he never allowed another person to take care of his most basic needs.

Walking out of the apartment, he wished once again there was a lock on the door. Until there was some security, it meant his M1911 was strapped to him twenty-four seven. He wasn't worried about Hannah getting hold of it. She was as harmless as they come. But until he knew who the tenant on the second floor was, he was going to stay on guard. *Hannah might trust you, but you're going to find I have one rule: trust is not given; it's earned.*

Outside of his men and his family, there was only one person he completely trusted. His best friend, Don Farrell, might not have joined the Navy with him, but he was one civilian he trusted with his life. Those first few years he'd come home from deployment Don had given him jobs working construction with him. *I was so lost and on edge. He gave me an outlet.* The man was brilliant and was one of the top construction engineers in the country. Everything he knew outside the Navy, he learned from Don. That was both good and bad. The guy was as unpredictable as they come. Don had no issue walking away from a successful career to start his own construction photography company. *One day he was building the skyscrapers and the next he was documenting the progress through photos.* Periodically Mark would work with Don between missions, but if he couldn't sit still long enough to handle a normal nine-to-five job, there was no way he could handle how quiet and boring it must be standing behind a camera all day. That's why he took this job in Savannah. Anything had sounded better than following Don around on a photo shoot. *Start taking pictures of models and you can count me in.*

This place wasn't lacking in beauty and charm, but it didn't make it on the excitement charts. At least in the city he was able to find something to occupy his time throughout the night. Here all he had was one stunning woman who was too young and sweet for his taste. That left only one thing. Work.

As he made his way across the lawn, he turned back to the house. Even though the curtains were drawn shut, he could tell the lights were on in the occupied apartment. Whoever the guy was, it was obvious he didn't sleep at night either. Was he just an early riser or was it something else? Everything Hannah had said already made him question the guy. If she didn't introduce them by Monday, he was going to find an excuse to do so himself.

Turning back to the shed, he opened the door, which instantly fell off its hinges. He had to catch it before it fell to the ground. *How is this place still standing?* Mark lifted the door and leaned it against the outside wall. *Don't let it cave in now.* The entire shed looked as though the elements had gotten to it. It was beyond only needing painted. He wasn't sure how long it'd been since someone had been inside, but it looked like a few years at least. *Add shed to the quickly growing list.*

Once inside, much to his surprise, he found it was well organized. Each tool sorted by type with all its accessories right by it. If this was her father's workshop, he was a man ready for anything. His collection was impressive. Mark's own father wasn't the repairman type. The most he'd seen in his father's tool box were a few screwdrivers and a hammer. If Don hadn't thrown him right into huge projects, he probably wouldn't know what half the equipment was in the shed. There was more than most people would normally have for basic home repairs. He picked up a few saws, and the blades and bits were worn enough to say the tools weren't just for show. *Shame to see them deteriorating with rust. But they're about to be put to good use very soon. There's no way I have what is needed in my Jeep. Actually, a wrecking ball might be more in order than a carpenter.*

He had no idea what shape the apartments were going to be in, but at least he knew he now had the tools to do whatever was necessary. All Mark needed to do was clean them off, and he was in business. Even Hannah's apartment needed some repairs but nothing outrageous from what he'd seen. Mostly fixing some floorboards, painting, and most important, *locks.* It was possible the others were in the same shape. If so, he was looking at a few weeks of work if he put in long days. Not that he wanted out of this place quickly, but he never let himself settle anywhere for very long.

Mark continued exploring the shed. Her father had

made great use of the space. Each cabinet he opened had more supplies than one could imagine. It was like her dad had his very own little hardware store tucked away in the boonies. There was everything from electrical and plumbing supplies to repair kits for walls and floors. He fished through as much as he could, hoping to find the one thing he wanted right now. *A damn lock.* Apparently, her father didn't seem concerned about them either as there wasn't a key or lock in sight. *This is about to change.*

When he left the shed, he took a look at the door still leaning where he'd put it. He was tempted to pull out a hammer and start working right where he was. The tenant might be up, but waking Hannah at that hour on a Sunday probably wasn't a great way to start their working relationship. *There are much better ways to wake someone like Hannah.*

There was no way he was heading back to the house with those thoughts in his mind. He wanted her. Who wouldn't? But Mark knew how to exercise self-control, and acting on sexual attraction for anything but short-term was a little like getting drunk—something to avoid. She was twenty-eight, and he was ten years her senior. Besides, she was not the type of woman he would hook up with. No matter how hard she tried to make him believe she was tough and fearless, he saw right through it. When he spoke about the door and her safety, he knew she not only needed someone to take care of her but yearned for it. Problem being, he was here but not for long. He would fix her home, make it secure, but he was not going to allow either of them to cross the line to anything other than that. She was already carrying pain; he didn't need to add to it.

HANNAH NORMALLY SLEPT like a log until a few weeks ago. Then she was tormented by something in her dreams, but couldn't remember what. It was frustrating waking each morning still tired from the night before and have no idea why. But last night she'd tossed and turned almost all night and her eyes barely closed. She tried telling herself it was the large iced coffee she drank that afternoon that kept her awake, but she knew better. It had been a long time since she'd been attracted to a man the way she was to Mark. He needed a haircut and a shave, but his body? *That* needed no improvement.

Having him stay in her apartment made the most sense as it was the most habitable. Giving him the apartment across from her that didn't have a working bathroom wasn't hospitable. So this was it. She'd need to hide the fact that she was melting inside each time he spoke. *His voice is so deep, so rich . . . sultry even.* He was here to do a job. And more importantly than her foolish lusty attraction, she needed him to do the job. Without him, she was going to lose the house to the bank. She only had a three month extension until they would come and put locks on the doors, and she wouldn't have a key. There was no way she'd let what her father had worked so hard to keep slip through her fingers. Getting involved with Mark in any way other than what repairs were needed was going to jeopardize that.

What's another few months of sexless living? It's already been years. I know it was sometime before I came home to care for Dad. Once I was here there was no time for a social life even if I wanted one. Maybe that's all it is with Mark. It's simply been too long.

Hannah opened her door and listened for any sound coming from his room. When she heard silence, she left the confines of her room and made her way to the kitchen. She'd spent the last hour watching the hands on the clock slowly move. Another minute in there and she was going to go crazy. She'd never lived alone until her father passed away. Her freshman year she shared a dorm room with her best friend, Bailey Tasca, and after that they decided to get their own apartment not from their school in Providence. Those had been some of the best times of her life. There was so much to do that she never sat home bored. You could go to a museum during the day and dance at a club that night. Things were open seven days a week.

Growing up with just her father in the house had been special, but she'd yearned for a female to be close to. Neighbors were not within walking distance, so the only time she saw her friends was at school. Funny how that was exactly what happened when she became an adult, she'd made a lifelong friend.

Thankfully Bailey still kept in contact. She'd even come down and stayed a week when her father died. She'd promised to go and visit her, but somehow things never worked out. At first, it was because she couldn't bring herself to be around anyone quite so happy all the time. And then it was because she didn't have the money to go. Bailey offered to pay her flight because she had a huge comedy improv competition coming up, but Hannah couldn't, or more accurately wouldn't, take a handout. It was bad enough she wasn't paying Mark anything close to what any other contractor would get paid. *I can only pay him what I make. And that's not much.*

As she poured herself a cup of coffee, she wondered why he was doing it. When she thought he was a retired man looking for work it seemed logical, but now it made no sense. *Even if he's out of work, what I'm paying is barely enough for a person to buy groceries, never mind put a roof over his head. What's your story, Mark Collins? I know you have one. I might just need to break my own rules about minding my own business and ask some questions. After all, you are staying in my house.*

As she went to sit down, she thought about heading back to her bedroom to have her coffee. Her robe was hanging on the back of the bathroom door and going out in her cami and pajama shorts wasn't the most modest thing to do, but it was better than the alternative. If she went for the robe, she knew the creaking of the bathroom door would surely wake Mark. She had no idea how late he liked to sleep, but she was a morning person. Like clockwork she got up, grabbed her coffee, and sat on the porch watching the sunrise with the birds.

With coffee in hand, she left her apartment and went to her favorite rocker. A book she'd been trying to read for the last month was on the table beside her, but once again she couldn't bring herself to open it. A love story only reminded her that happily ever after was not for her. *I should start reading mysteries. Maybe then I'll start being paranoid like Mark.* Hannah laughed to herself.

"Someone is happy this morning."

His deep voice startled her. Because she didn't want to attract bugs, she'd left the porch light off. Now she could hear but not see him. Had he been there watching her all this time? *No. If I can't see him, then he can't see me. No need to be self-conscious. I just need to go in the house before him and book it to my room.*

"Yes, I am. Have a good day, Mr. Collins." She got off her rocking chair and headed for the door. Before she could open it, he spoke again.

"Pink suits you."

Damn. Hannah grabbed the doorknob, pulled it open, and quickly went inside. She might not be able to see him, but clearly, he could see her.

When she got to her bedroom, she slammed the door shut. *Maybe Mark was right. I should've asked a lot more questions before letting him into my house. He obviously doesn't understand how to respect someone's privacy. God, he could've turned and looked the other way. But no. He watched me. Why?*

Hannah pulled a pair of jeans over her shorts and a T-shirt over her cami. She didn't even take time to brush her hair. All she wanted to do right now was give him a piece of her mind.

She opened her door and headed back to the porch. This time she turned on the light. She wanted to meet his eyes when she told him what a creepy thing that was to do. When she got to the porch, he was sitting at the far end in what was her father's favorite spot. Her growing anger choked in her throat at the sight. All she could picture was her father sitting there. Yelling at Mark in that seat wasn't something she could do.

"Mr. Collins, I would like to speak to you in the kitchen." She didn't wait for a response and left him alone on the porch. If he didn't follow her then she knew no matter how badly she needed him here to do the work, she would send him packing today.

As she stood in the kitchen, she realized she'd been holding her breath until he entered.

"You're angry," Mark said as he came to stand by her.

She crossed her arms in front of her, half to make a statement and the other half to cover the fact she hadn't put on a bra. "Shouldn't I be? I mean you invaded my privacy."

"No. I didn't."

"Of course, you did. I was sitting on my porch, and you were sitting there watching me." Even as she said it, she became angry all over again.

"First of all, I was already sitting on the porch when you came out. So you cannot claim I invaded your privacy."

"I didn't know you were there."

"And that changes what exactly? If you did, would you have gone back and put on a robe? Or would you have still come out on the porch?"

She didn't answer him.

"You know you don't live here alone. You're lucky it was me there and not your tenant. What if he would've been there watching you? At least, I made my presence known. That was a choice. I didn't have to."

"I would've heard you eventually."

"Only if I wanted you to," Mark stated in a tone which clearly said he wasn't joking.

Was he threatening her? Was that some type of warning of what he could do to her if he wanted? She looked into his eyes and saw he wasn't a man to challenge, but there was something more. Was it gentleness? No, it couldn't be. Nothing about him looked anything but fierce, powerful, and intimidating as hell. Although Sissie had mentioned how protective he was of his younger sister, she thought that was normal from a big brother, but he wasn't her family or her friend. *Thanks for scaring me in my own home. That so isn't on your list.* "What are you saying? That you can—"

"That you need damn locks on your doors, and stop thinking you're safe here. If you don't, someday you're going to meet someone who won't be a gentleman like me. Understood?"

Mark barked at her and she trembled. What had just

occurred did open her eyes. She didn't want the rose-colored glasses removed. It was all she had right now, and she needed them more than he understood. Someone like him, who saw danger around every corner, would never or could never understand. But he was right. She was going to have to make a few changes in this place. Locks could be the first priority. The other was keeping her distance from him.

"Okay. Lock first thing tomorrow. Anything else?"

"Yes. For God's sake, stop calling me Mr. Collins. Call me Mark or call me Collins. And don't you dare call me sir either."

So full of requests so bright and early. Maybe I should learn to sleep in from now on. But why on earth would I call him sir? He's not that old. Men.

"Fine. If you'll excuse me, Mark, I have something I need to attend to." *Don't know what it is, but it's not here with you.* She walked out of the kitchen and headed toward her bedroom. Once inside she leaned against the closed door. "Please let him get these repairs done fast. I'm not going to be able to do this every day."

CHAPTER THREE

HANNAH DIDN'T MAKE the same mistake on Monday morning. She had her robe on any time she left the confines of her bedroom. Mark seemed to agree that the less they spoke about the porch incident, the better.

Even before she entered the kitchen, the aroma caught her attention. Someone was cooking bacon. She knew everything in her refrigerator, and that wasn't one of the items. Stores weren't open yet either. So where did he get bacon at this early hour?

Her nose hadn't lied. Mark was standing at the stove wearing a tight T-shirt and jeans that hugged his butt. *The food's not the only thing delicious in here.* She could see the strings from her apron tied around his waist. Hannah couldn't figure this man out. Hard as nails yet comfortable enough to slap on a frilly apron while cooking. It was tempting to pinch herself to make sure she was, in fact, awake. *This picture is definitely something I would dream about. Except he would only be wearing my apron. But only because cooking without an apron can be hazardous. Don't want any vital parts getting burned.* A dirty little smile crossed her face.

She couldn't pull her eyes off him. His shoulders were broad and tapered to a trim waist that ended with a butt made to grab. *God, that man's butt was made for jeans.* Tipping her head slightly for an even better view, she couldn't help but grin as she bit her lip, holding back laughter as not to make her presence known. *With a body like that, let's lose the apron too.*

"Good morning, Hannah."

He didn't even turn around, yet he still greeted her as though he knew she was there. But did he know her thoughts were hot enough to sizzle the bacon?

"Good . . . good morning, Mark. Bacon?"

"Fresh from the farm."

"Care to elaborate?"

"Went for an early morning run and met one of your neighbors."

She was far from town. Her closest neighbor was at least ten miles away. That's not a run. That's more like a marathon. "Do you mean the Hagers?"

"You mean Gerald and Patty?"

Day three and already on a first-name basis with the locals? We're friendly but not that open. This was her hometown, and she'd never called them anything but Mr. and Mrs. Hager. *Who are you, Mark Collins?*

"And the bacon?"

Mark finally turned from the stove and faced her. "Guess I looked hungry." Mark laughed. *Oh. Good. God.*

Her jaw almost dropped. *He's gorgeous.* He not only had cut his hair short, but he was clean shaven. *You're making me hungry, Mark Collins, like I've never been hungry before. I already have so much on my mind. Day-dreaming of you kissing me, touching me, isn't going to help any.*

Hannah turned away before he could see the desire in her eyes. "Hope they gave you enough for two because I'm starving."

There was no way was she going to let him get to her. *Where do they grow men like him? And more importantly, what bad have I done in my life that he would turn up in my house, when there is no possible chance I can do anything with him? Stay focused. He's here to repair the house. Not your broken libido.* They had a long day ahead of them. First, do a walk through the apartments to see what supplies were needed and then go into town and hopefully have enough money to get the supplies. "What can I do to help?"

"Pour some coffee and have a seat. But don't get used to my cooking. It's not in my contract."

She smiled as she walked up to grab a coffee cup from the cupboard next to him. "Is it too late to renegotiate?"

The light banter back and forth was refreshing. Whatever friction had been there yesterday was gone. *It's in the past,* and she was going to leave it there. If only she could do the same with the sexual attraction she felt for him. Her arm barely brushed against his, and her body warmed. What was it that made every nerve in her come to life? It'd been a long time since she'd felt an intimate touch, too long, but this was beyond anything she'd experienced before. She wanted it to stop, yet she wanted it to never end.

Her hand trembled as she poured the dark liquid into her cup. She wasn't going to criticize, but it didn't look anything like what she made. Hannah drank her coffee black, but this looked like it was going to require some doctoring. Too bad she didn't have any cream. She brought the cup to her mouth, took one sip, and almost spit it out. He must've seen the look on her face that screamed *horrible.*

"Sorry. I should've warned you. I make it strong."

Caffeine in the morning was a necessity, but today she was going to pass on that. Putting the full cup on the counter, Hannah jokingly said, "If I end up growing hair on my chest, I'm blaming you."

Mark gave her a wink. "That's the last pot of coffee I brew. I don't want to be responsible for ruining anything so perfect."

Hannah felt her cheeks warm at his sweet little flirt. She'd seen him eyeing her before. But to hear him verbalize that he liked what he saw made her heart race. *Please stop looking at me like that.* She didn't respond to him. Instead she turned to the cupboard again and pulled some plates down.

"If I can't help cook, then I'll set the table." As she was placing the dishes on the table, she could feel him watching her, probably like he'd felt her watching him earlier. This was a habit they couldn't afford to start. One thing was going to lead to another and the only building that was going to get done was building passion. *Sweet, but not productive.* "Don't let that bacon burn," Hannah said to get his attention back to where it belonged.

She heard him laugh softly then scrape the metal tongs against the cast iron pan.

Thankfully they were able to keep the topic purely business over breakfast. "You cooked, so I'll do the dishes."

He ignored her and continued washing the pans he used to cook earlier. Not only was he doing the ones from that morning, but she noticed what she'd left there the night before had been already done as well.

"Mark, I can—"

"And so can I."

He was a man obviously used to being in control. She was used to having to do everything herself. Besides her father, no other person had ever stopped to take care of her in any way. If anything she was the one always doing for everyone. Here was a man who appeared out of nowhere, asking her to do what was so unfamiliar to her. *Let go.*

It was stupid. They were only dirty dishes, so why did she want to get up and force the issue that she could do them herself? *Because he's only here for a short time. If I let him do for me now, it will only be worse when he leaves.*

I have to remember that I can't miss what I never had.

She picked up her plate and walked to stand by Mark. She slipped it into the soapy water. Even though it was awkward because she needed to lean over, she put her hand into the water, grabbed the second sponge, and started washing the plate. Mark didn't budge.

"Stubborn, aren't you?" he asked, towering over her.

His body was warm against hers. It would be so easy to give in, not to just dishes either. Instead she nudged him with her hip, not making eye contact. "More than you know. I'll wash, you dry."

He didn't move at first, but then she felt his body relax and step to the right, giving her full access to the sink. Not that she liked washing dishes, but this morning she found it something she didn't mind one bit. It didn't take long before everything was put back in place.

"Are you going to be hovering over me like this when I start the work on the house?"

Hannah laughed. "I can deal with a broken plate or cup. But if you think this house is in need of repair now, you don't want to see what would happen if you let me near a power tool."

"For all you know, I'm not any better."

Oh, you probably could drive a nail into a board with your bare hand. Those are working man hands. Strong. Powerful. Damn I want to feel them on me. She cleared her throat. "Then you better tell me now before we head to town and pick up supplies."

"Don't worry your pretty little head. I'm very good

with my hands."

She didn't miss the curl of his lips as he spoke. *Just keep them where they belong. A sample of what you're offering will open a gate I may not be able to close afterward. If I think I feel alone now, it would be one hundred times worse when you leave.* That thought confused her. She was used to being alone. When her father was sick and spent a lot of time sleeping, she was always alone. She had felt alone at times but not lonely. But in the year since his death, that had morphed into *loneliness. Am I feeling this way just because he is the first man to banter with me in years?* She had to stop thinking about this. Mark Collins was a temporary person in her life, here to do a job, then move on to the next.

"Let's take a tour of the empty apartments and head to town." She wiped her wet hands on the towel and left the kitchen. Distance was what she needed right now. *And maybe a cold shower.*

MARK TOOK NOTES of all the work needed on the empty apartments. Since she was going to show the top right one at the end of the week, he figured that was where he needed to start. What he hadn't expected was the amount of work left. No plumbing hooked up in the kitchen or the bathroom. It was convenient that there also wasn't a floor in the bathroom yet. What she was asking to happen couldn't be done in a few days by one person. Even two wasn't going to be easy. *Going to deliver some bad news. Hope she's ready for the truth, 'cause that's all I deal in.*

"Better cancel your appointment. There is no way this is going to be ready by Friday."

"I thought you said you were good with your hands?"

"I am." He held them up. "If you notice, I only have two. What you need done to make it safe for someone to walk through will take at least two people. That doesn't count getting it all pretty looking with paint. That's making it safe."

He saw the look on her face. Of course, she was disappointed. Who wouldn't be? But she wasn't living in reality if she thought for one minute this could work.

"You don't understand. It can't wait, Mark. I need. . . I have to. . ." She turned away and walked to an open window, standing there quietly.

You're right; I don't understand. So tell me. "What do you need, Hannah?"

Still not facing him, she sighed heavily. "I need the income."

Money. It isn't always about money. "It's one month at the most."

"One month that determines if I have this place or not. I can't afford to lose that money, Mark. Without it, the bank will foreclose on the house. This is only an old house to you, nothing more. But not to me. If the bank takes it, then I'll have failed and lost the only thing I have left of my father."

Her voice was soft as she spoke, but he could feel how voicing the words out loud brought her immense pain. He'd known things had to be financially tight when he heard what he'd be paid. Practically room and board. If he smoked or drank, maybe enough to cover that as well. But he wasn't there for the money. He was there for his sanity. He could walk away now and find another place to decompress, but leaving her, knowing she was going to lose her home, would haunt him.

Mark could easily open his wallet and give her the money to float this place several months. But he'd only hurt her pride, which he knew she had in spades given her refusal to let him do her dishes. There was so much more to her than her pride. He could tell she put on one hell of a front that she was tough and independent, but he could see deep inside she was shaking and needed someone to lean on. He wanted to go to her, wrap his arms around her, and tell her she wasn't alone. He was here. He'd help her with whatever she needed. But the truth was, he wasn't that person. She could lean on him now, but once he got that call, she would find herself exactly where she was today. *Alone.*

Think, Collins. Can't call in the team for this. They need their R&R as much as I do. And if I get called so will they. I need someone I can trust totally. And a damn good plan so she doesn't think this is charity. She needs to continue to think she's the one in control.

He knew exactly who that was. There was only one problem. Don was far from a guy in need of a handout. Bringing him here was going to require a long private talk and a lot of luck that he was between contracts.

"I won't let that happen, Hannah, but you might need to provide another room for a guy I know who is a bit down and out on his luck right now. But he knows his way around construction better than anyone I know."

Even from the back, he saw her wipe her cheeks before she turned to face him. "You think he'll really be willing to help me?"

For me, yes. "I would consider it more like you're helping him." *The man needs to get out of the city for a while. Besides, it's been way too long since we worked on a project. It'll give us time to catch up.*

"I can only offer the same thing I've offered you."

Her beautiful green eyes, still glistening from the tears, were filled with hope. There was no way he was going to disappoint her. Soon as he got a minute alone, he was going to reach out to Don with the plan. *He's never let me down before. I know if I get the call, he'll at least see this through without me.*

"Why don't I meet you at my Jeep, and I'll see if I can reach him."

She smiled and went to walk past him but stopped, and with her tiny soft hand touched his forearm. "Thank you, Mark. I don't know what I would've done if you hadn't—"

"Just doing my job."

She nodded and let go. "Thanks." Then she left him alone in the empty apartment.

The last thing he needed was her feeling endeared to him in any way. He wasn't worried about his acting skills. God knows he'd used them so many times overseas that he'd lost count. It was easier playing whatever role he needed to, rather than being himself most times. Now he just had to make sure Don was up to the task as well.

Once she was out of earshot, he pulled out his cell and dialed Farrell.

"It's been a while, Collins. Where you been hiding?"

Don knew he could ask but wouldn't be told. "Around. I'm actually calling for a favor."

"Looking for work? I thought you didn't want to get behind a camera."

"Actually, I think it's time you took a vacation."

"Hell yeah. Where are we off to? Rio? St Lucia? Dubai? Monte Carlo?"

"Savannah, Georgia."

"Did they get a topless beach I haven't heard about? 'Cause that doesn't seem like my type of vacation," Don said while laughing.

"Plan on being without a shirt, because the air conditioner isn't working here either." *Put update the electrical on the endless list.*

"Mark, what exactly is this favor? I think I've just become busy."

He knew Don was only joking. They've never said no to any request before unless it truly couldn't happen. "There's this woman Hannah Entwistle—"

"Ah. Now you have my attention. Tell me more."

Don't make it what it isn't. "She is about to lose her family home if we can't pull off a miracle and get it fixed up so she can rent the place by the end of the month."

"Why don't you just give her the money or pay someone to do it?"

"If I thought for one minute she'd accept it, I would."

"And you care about this why?"

"I only want to help her. She has nothing but this place." Don would understand once he met her. It was impossible to explain over the phone.

"So what do you want from me?"

"I need you to fly out here and pretend you're out of work and willing to do the job for room and board."

Don laughed. "Do I get a bed or am I sleeping in a tree somewhere?"

"Just get here. This place is falling apart around her. She has the tools but nothing else. Oh, I need you to reach out to the hardware store and have them extend her credit. And by that I mean—"

"Yeah, I know how this works, Mark. I will make sure all is quiet, and it won't lead back to you. Anything else?"

"I need you to find me a contact for the bank that holds her mortgage."

"How do you think you're going to keep that one from her if they already gave her notice?"

"Let me worry about that. So when are you going to get here?"

"I can have my jet there tonight."

"Don, I don't care if you fly by private jet, but remember, you're broke."

Don laughed again. "Fine. I won't shave today and might even skip a shower. Will that do?"

"I really need your help, and we don't want to scare her, so please, shower." Before he disconnected the call, he said, "I really owe you, Don."

"Collins, if you get all mushy on me I'm not showing up. Now text the damn information to where the hell I'm going and any personal information you think I might need. I'll see you tonight."

One down, one to go. He put the phone back in his pocket and went to meet Hannah. She was standing on the porch waiting for him.

"Were you able to reach your friend?"

She still looked worried. Since she had no clue what really was going on, she should be worried.

"Yeah. He's bumming a ride and will be here sometime late tonight."

"That's wonderful. Did you make the list of what we need at the store?"

If by list you mean the entire store, then yes. "What we don't grab today, I'll grab with Don tomorrow."

"I just want to make sure we only get what is absolutely necessary."

A construction crew and a miracle is what you absolutely need. But what you've got is me and the one man who can help me pull it off. "Don't worry. I'm used to working with little. When we're done, you'll be shocked at what you see." *Just don't ask too many questions on how exactly we pull it off. Lying is not something I enjoy doing, but if it's necessary for safety, or in this case, a beautiful woman's hope, I will.*

"Let's get going."

Mark headed towards his Jeep.

"Let's take my car."

He raised a brow. "We're picking up supplies that you might not want in your fancy convertible."

She looked at her Volkswagen then at his Jeep. "Good point. But then again, I don't want to end up walking back because we break down either." Hannah pulled her keys out of her purse waving them in the air as she hopped into the driver's seat. "We can talk on the way, and you can tell me all about yourself."

That's not going to happen. "I think I'd much rather hear about you and Savannah. I've never been here before. Why don't you tell me about it?"

He was good about making sure no one knew anything about him except those closest to him. Even then, they only knew what he was willing or able to share. Most of his life was top secret. Where he was and what he was doing never could be discussed. Not even his parents knew. It wasn't always the easiest life, but it was the one he wanted, the one he chose.

After they returned from the store, Mark installed the lock on her apartment door. Then a second one on her bedroom door. She looked at him like she was about to dispute that, but said nothing. *Progress. Baby steps, but progress.*

Hannah had shown Mark a room for Don then went to bed early by his standards. He was glad she didn't stay up waiting to meet him. He needed to discuss with Don what actually was going on, away from Hannah's ears. Especially after the conversation he'd had with the bank earlier.

It hadn't taken Don long to get the bank contact information. The rest had been left to Mark to handle. It was convenient that she used a local bank which meant dealing with people who were in charge and could make decisions. The one problem with that was a small town meant people knew and said more than they should. Mark was able to obtain the information regarding how far behind she was on her mortgage as well as why.

She'd been struggling for longer than he'd thought, taking on debts that weren't hers, and never taking a handout of any kind. *Sweet, stubborn Hannah. You may think you won the battle, but trust me, I'll win the war.* Her unwillingness to accept his help wasn't going to happen. Many people might let that deter them, but he never let anything come between him and a successful mission. *And saving your family home has just become my personal mission.*

Don pulled up in an old beat-up truck. "Where the hell did you get that?"

"You said I'd be working for peanuts, so I bought this off a peanut farmer the next town over. What do you think?"

That you're nuts. "It suits you. You should drive it

more often," Mark said while laughing.

Don pointed to the Jeep. "Is that why you took Bessy on this road trip?"

"You know she and I go way back."

"Yeah, too long if you ask me. Every time I see you pull up in that green thing you call a vehicle I cringe."

"You're just jealous because you rolled yours when we went four-wheeling."

"That was a damn good time. Sounds like a better vacation than what you have planned for me here. Want to talk while we can?"

You know it. "Did you get things set up at the hardware store?"

"That's why I'm here so late."

Not the only reason I'm sure. "Excellent. We're going to need it. Don, you've no idea what work we have ahead of us."

"Worse than the last job we did in Buffalo together?"

"Makes it look like a walk in the park."

"Tell me again why we're not using a crew?"

"Because I don't want her to know we're funding this."

Don shook his head. "So you think she's going to believe that the two of us are so hard up on our luck that we're willing to do all this work for room and board only? And that the store is running one hell of a special deal right now, and her supplies are dirt cheap?"

Not when you say it like that. "Leave that to me. You're here to make sure it can be pulled off. If anyone can make this place livable, it's you."

"Great. No pressure."

That's what was nice about having Don help. They might not have worked together on any projects for the last three years, but it was like old times as soon as they connected. He wouldn't bring additional stress. In fact having him around meant one less thing Mark needed to worry about. *Don is someone who will ask questions, but not flip out if he isn't given any answers.*

Mark and Don sat on the porch far from the door in case Hannah decided to come out and join them. The last thing he needed was for her to overhear their conversation. She already wasn't going to be happy, but Mark planned on being long gone before she caught on to what transpired. It was going to be too late by then.

He informed Don what the bank said. "Even if she fixes this place up she might lose it? So what's the point? Just tell her the truth and be done with it."

"Don. She lost her father about a year ago. I know we see a money pit, but this was . . . is her family's home. When she talked about it, I could see she wasn't ready to let go yet. And I'm not going to let a bank or anyone else tell her she has to before she's ready. Hannah needs someone to fight for her, even if she doesn't want to admit it."

Don looked at him questioningly. "You of all people know you can't save everyone."

It was something he lived with every day of his life. He'd lost members of his team as well as too many others he'd met in the field. Over the years you would think you'd stop counting, but you don't. Each one had a name, a family, a story. He refused to let any of them be forgotten. *I might not be able to save them all, but I sure as hell am going to try.*

"Don, this is different."

"You're right. You're not on a battlefield somewhere. And this is not your men that you can order around. Hate to tell you, buddy, but you're trying to control this, and you can't do that when it comes to women. They have a knack for finding out, and when she does, it'll be hell to pay."

One fragile woman doesn't scare me. "Trust me, Don. I know what I'm doing."

"I'm only here to work and watch the show," Don joked. "I do know one thing."

"What's that?"

Don slapped Mark on the back. "I can't wait to meet this woman. Whoever she is, she sure has shaken you up."

Mark didn't get shaken by anything or anyone. He was task-driven and right now helping her was just that, the task at hand. "I feel for her situation, Don. Nothing more."

"So what you're saying is she's available? Maybe this vacation won't be so bad after all." Don arched his brow, taunting Mark.

Even though he knew Don was just joking, his gut tied in a knot. "What I'm saying is you can sleep in that tree or the old piece of shit truck you drove up here in, but keep your hands off Hannah."

Don burst out laughing. "Don't worry, Mark. I won't touch your girl." *My girl? Hannah could never be my girl.*

The problem with bringing his best friend in was he'd never hear the end of it. "Keep it up and you'll—"

Don got up and said, "Be sleeping on this porch. Yeah, I know already. Want to show me where I'm really sleeping? If I'm right, you're going to get my ass up before the birds."

Damn straight. Mark got up and headed for the door. "You've got a room in the empty apartment across from ours."

"Ours?" Don joked again.

Fuck. "Don't make me regret calling you, Don."

He was still laughing as he entered the house.

"And keep it down. Hannah's sleeping."

"You're making this too easy. But don't worry, Mark. I walked away from one hell of a deal to be here, and you better believe I'm going to get some enjoyment out of it."

Mark knew it wasn't about money. It was payback for something he'd done to Don all the way back in high school. That man had a memory that was unheard of. His revenge always caught Mark by surprise. Usually harmless fun. But Don sending a letter to his mother informing her he had gotten married overseas and was coming home with triplet babies might've been going too far. Ever since that day Mark's mother said he owed her three grandchildren, and she wasn't going to rest until he paid up. Whatever Don had in store for him this time better not include Hannah. She had enough going on in her life already. The last thing she needed was Don Farrell adding anything to it.

"Get your sleep, Don. Tomorrow you have to earn your keep. And when you see the apartment upstairs, you're going to understand why I called."

"That bad?"

"I'm still trying to find what I like about it."

"Who's in the other one?"

"Not sure. I've been here since Saturday and haven't seen him at all. No lights on during the day, but he's up all night moving around. Something is off about that guy."

"And you know this how?"

His job was observing suspicious behaviors. "Trust me. I know. Your bedroom is right beneath his. Keep your ears open and text me if anything seems off to you."

"What exactly am I supposed to be listening for?"

Mark had no clue. The hairs on the back of his neck stood up each time he thought of the guy. That wasn't much to go on, but that was enough for now. He'd learned years ago to listen to his gut. And his gut was saying something was not right.

"Don, just text me if you hear anything at all."

"So you're expecting me to stay up all night? Is there anything else you want to tell me about this lovely vacation?"

Mark turned to leave Don alone but shot over his shoulder, "Yeah, the coffee here is like water."

CHAPTER FOUR

HANNAH WOKE EARLY to hear loud banging echoing through the house. She reached for her cell phone. *Really? Six a.m.*

The noise was only half the issue. She'd been having the most amazing dream of Mark before being so rudely awoken. Closing her eyes, she still pictured him clearly. He'd been outside chopping wood as she watched him from the porch. The heat of the day was getting to him. Slowly he ripped off his shirt, exposing beautiful ripples of muscles. Bending down to pick up the water hose, he raised it overhead and doused himself. As the water flowed over his body, she wished it was her hands and her mouth.

Hannah could feel the desire still aching for attention. *Horny and wet for a man I can't have. This is going to be a long day.*

She was about to pull the sheets over her head and try going back to sleep when she heard a power saw cutting something in the room right above hers. *Just because he doesn't like to sleep, doesn't mean the rest of the world shouldn't.*

She threw the sheet off to one side, dragged herself from the bed, and stomped across the floor. Normally she was lighter on her feet as she liked things quiet, but this morning no amount of noise she made would compare to the racket going on upstairs.

She grabbed her thin cotton robe hanging on the back of her door. It didn't cover much more than the tiny pajama set she was wearing, but she was too angry to think about modesty at the moment. She didn't even bother combing her hair. There was no way she'd allow Mark to wake her tenant at that godawful hour. The last thing she needed was him to complain and move out due to the noise. She hadn't let him know about the construction yet. *Bad on me, but who would've thought they'd start at pre-dawn?*

Leaving her apartment, she climbed the stairs to the vacant apartment. Hannah was thankful her tenant wasn't directly below the construction like she was, but she was sure it was echoing throughout the house. Each step brought her closer, and she couldn't wait to give Mark a piece of her mind. *No matter how sexy you are to look at, nothing is going to stop me from saying what's on my mind.*

When she arrived, she found the apartment wide open. She marched right in, but after a few steps she stopped dead in her tracks. Mark was standing with his back to her, his arms above his head holding what looked like a wooden beam of some sort. Hannah wasn't too interested in what he was holding. He was shirtless, and every muscle in his arms and back was calling out to her. If that wasn't bad enough, his tool belt was tugging on his jeans, bringing them even lower over that fine-looking ass of his. *Even sweeter than my dream.*

She could stand there forever and look at him. Her eyes burned the memory of him in her mind. It took everything within her not to reach out and touch him. Any anger she'd felt on her way upstairs was quickly replaced with raw, uncontrollable need. Her feet were defying what her head knew she should do—turn and go back downstairs and pretend she never saw all that sexiness. But her brain wasn't in control. One step, then two. Closer and closer to what she yearned for.

"Hurry the fuck up, Don. This thing isn't holding itself up over here."

Oh, God. He knows someone is here. How does he do that? She took a step backward. *At least, he doesn't know it's me.*

Hannah blushed and couldn't even believe what she'd been about to do. Did she really think she'd walk over and touch him without him noticing? *Who am I kidding? There is no way I'm going to be able to stop with one touch. Maybe after a kiss and, oh yeah, a lick or two.*

Hannah was so deep in her own thoughts as she backed up almost to the doorway, that she wasn't paying attention to any of her surroundings, except for Mark. She caught the back of her heel on something, sending her tumbling to the floor.

"Ow!" The word escaped her lips, barely a whisper as she covered her mouth so not to be heard.

Instantly Mark spun around, and the one chance to slip out had slipped away. The beam he was holding came crashing to the floor as he moved quickly to her side.

"Are you okay?" He was looking her over as though he expected some serious injury.

The only thing hurt was her pride. "Ow." She could feel several things poking into her all at the same time. Her hand went to feel what it could be when she picked up a nail. Then she looked by her foot and saw a plastic bucket tipped over and an empty box of nails. *Great. With everything in this room, I have to not just knock it over but scatter nails all over the floor. If it wasn't for bad luck right now, I don't think I would have any luck at all.* She moved a bit and something dug into her. She winced. *Lucky me, I'm on a bed of nails. How am I going to get off this without hurting more than just my pride? Heck, it hurts just sitting on it.*

Her short robe now wide open revealed more than she wanted. *It's not the first time you've seen me like this, but this time I know you can see everything. There is no darkness hiding me this time. Can this get any worse?*

"I'm fine. Just let me get up." She needed him to back away. Her body hadn't recovered from the sight of him, so his closeness was only keeping the flame lit.

"No. I'll pick you up."

Before she could argue with him, his strong arms

were beneath her, lifting her up against his bare chest. *Got my wish. Not the way I saw this happening, but I got to touch you. Even in this awkward situation, you feel amazing.* He was hot and hard, such a sweet contrast to her cold soft hands. She wasn't sure if she should laugh or cry at how pathetic this all was. It was like a scene from a love story. If only it were true, his lips would soon claim hers in a passionate, explosive kiss.

Before either of them spoke, a deep voice from behind her said, "You must be the lovely Hannah Mark has been talking about."

She turned her head to find a man almost as tall and about the same age as Mark. Unlike Mark, though, this man was all mischievous smiles. Hannah had no doubt why. They were caught in a very compromising situation—both Mark and she were half dressed.

"Don't mind my friend Mark. It seems having his hands full has made him lose his manners. I'm Don Farrell, Mark's helper for a while."

She felt Mark tense. This wasn't any more pleasant for her, yet he didn't put her down. The more she tried pulling away, the more it was obvious her attempts were totally ineffective. His arms were like steel. *Beautiful pillars of hot steel.* Her cheeks burned with embarrassment. Even with another person in the room, she couldn't control her dirty little thoughts.

"Will you please put me down?"

Mark slowly let her legs drop to the floor, but he continued to hold her against him with his other arm.

"All the way," she demanded without meeting his eyes. Her hand had already felt his heart pounding. There was no need to confirm what she felt by seeing the same desire burning in his eyes.

Once freed she headed for the door. Don gave her a sweet nod and stepped out of her way. As she passed, he gave her a playful wink. *Are you sure you two are friends? You're as different as night and day.*

Before she made it out the door, Mark had swooped her back up into his arms.

"What are you doing? Put me down!"

This time she pushed against his chest and shoulders, but the outcome was the same.

"Stop wiggling. You're hurt."

Hannah froze as she tried to assess her body. She didn't feel any pain. Was this some ploy? If so it so wasn't funny. "I'm fine," she informed him firmly.

"You're bleeding. I need to get you to your apartment and get your clothes off."

Good try. "I am not that naïve, Mr. Collins. So I am only going to say this one more time before I show you my southern temper. Put me down!"

Mark stared at her, challenging her to do so. "Do you honestly think I'd hurt you?"

She wasn't sure. There *was* something dangerous about him. When she looked in his eyes, it was there, even though he tried to hide it. When she didn't answer, he continued.

"Who do you think would come to your rescue?

Your tenant? Don?"

The tenant was not an option, but she wasn't so sure about Don. Turning her head so she could see him, he only shrugged at her.

"Above my pay grade."

Hannah couldn't believe the man could joke at a time like this. She was being manhandled, and no one was going to do anything to stop it. *What if I really was in trouble? Who'd call the police? He was right. Anything could happen to me out here, and there's no one to save me.*

Her screaming was only a threat, and he'd called her bluff. *So let's try plan B.*

"Mark, I appreciate you trying to help me, but I assure you I can take care of myself. I'm fine."

As he held her with one arm, his free hand rubbed her bottom gently. Any other time, and in private, she would most certainly enjoy *that*, but this was not happening.

When he pulled his hand up, he held it so she could see. *Blood. Oh, my God. I'm bleeding.*

"That's . . . blo—"

"As I said, you're hurt. I need to see how bad. So either you're going to let me look at you here in front of Don, or we can do it downstairs in your room. But understand this, Hannah, these are your only two options."

I'm bleeding. Panic filled her, and Mark must have sensed it.

"Move, Don," Mark barked at his friend who gave

way for them to pass.

Within seconds, they were inside her apartment, and she was standing on her bedroom floor.

"I need to go to the bathroom so I can see where I'm bleeding in the mirror."

He didn't move out of her way. Instead Mark reached out took off the light cotton robe and tossed it to the side.

"I can take care of myself." She wasn't used to anyone taking such control over her in this manner. Yes she may be injured, but she wasn't an invalid.

"Turn around so I can take a look."

She was once again in her tiny shorts and cami. It wasn't naked but too damn close for her to feel comfortable standing there with him staring at her. "Get me a mirror and I will look."

"You will not be able to see if it is a puncture wound or a scratch from a mirror. Now turn around and let me look."

This house isn't worth all this humiliation. Slowly she turned. Hannah could feel his warm fingers gently lift the bottom of her cami up, so it was in the middle of her back. Then even more gently he slid her shorts down.

I could just die. This can't be happening. My fantasies never included any of this.

His hands now touched her bare bottom, not in a sensual way, but as though he was medical professional.

"I need to clean away the blood. Do you have any hydrogen-peroxide or an antibacterial cleanser?"

"No."

"How about rubbing alcohol?"

Her eyes widened and tried to turn to face him. "That's going to hurt."

"It will. But I have to clean the cut, or it could get infected. It looks like a small puncture wound, and you won't need stitches, but that doesn't mean I don't have to clean it."

Everything in his tone was one of control and professionalism as though he'd done this a hundred times before, but his touch was so gentle. *What type of contractor are you that you're so comfortable doing this? I know guys get hurt on the job, but you're so in control, like this is second nature to you.* Hannah didn't want to tell him where the alcohol was, but he was correct. It had to be cleaned. If she didn't let him do it, then she would need to go to the hospital. Things were bad enough without medical bills.

She hadn't used the alcohol since her father had passed away. He'd had some medical equipment that needed to be kept clean. Never did she think it'd be used on her.

"Soap and water?" Even as she said it, she knew what his answer was going to be. But she had to try. He didn't even bother to shake his head.

Arguing with you is as useless as trying to get out of your arms. Damn, you're stubborn. Unfortunately, you're also right. "It's in the medicine cabinet."

He grabbed the bottle and moved them to the bedroom, then he said, "Lay down on your stomach."

"I'm okay standing."

"Do you want this done right? Or do you want a trip to the emergency room?"

You really know what to say to get me to do what you want. It's like bossy is your default. It's kind of hot, but not right now. Hot? Really? Even in this situation I'm thinking he's hot? Maybe they have a shot for these insane thoughts running through my mind.

Before she laid upon her bed, Mark placed a towel down to protect her sheets. If it were any other circumstance, she'd appreciate his thoughtfulness. But she didn't care about sheets or shorts or anything else. All she could think was her bare butt was only inches away from his face. *Don't think of that. Think medical bills. Think of how foolish you were in the first place for entering the room. Think about . . . how he looked when he was holding up the beam. Every muscle defined. And how his biceps felt when he carried yo*— "Ow! Sweet Jesus! Ow!" He continued to wipe the open cut with the alcohol-soaked cloth. "Are you trying to kill me?"

The burning was worse than she'd expected but no matter how she protested or tried to stop him, he held her in place and continued to clean the wound.

"Almost done."

When she thought she couldn't take any more, the torture ended. She didn't remember when she stopped yelling at him and began sobbing, but her face was buried in her wet palms. It wasn't just the pain. Everything seemed to be crashing down on her all at once. Getting hurt was just the icing on the cake.

Hannah hadn't allowed herself to cry when her father died. She'd told herself to be strong. But the truth was she was tired of always being strong. Everything fell on her shoulders and the weight seemed unbearable now. *I should give up. Walk away. Dad would understand. I am not strong enough. Never have been and never will be.*

The tears flowed harder, and her body began to rock with sobs.

The hands that brought such pain stroked her back gently. Mark had somehow come to lie beside her. He pulled her up against him, so she now lay half on him with her head on his chest.

"Sorry, baby. I didn't mean to hurt you. It's over."

No. It's not. It's far from over. As long as I'm here, it never will be. Hannah didn't want to hold on to him. She wanted him out. Wanted to be alone. Yet she found herself clinging to him as she cried.

Dad. Please forgive me. I can't do it. I don't know how, and no matter how hard I try, the result will be the same. I'm going to lose this house and everything you worked for. You always thought I was stronger than I actually am. Why did you think I could do all this by myself? She couldn't bear disappointing him. It had been his dying request that she keep the house, and one day raise a family of her own there. It was his dream, not hers, but she agreed, and now she couldn't bring herself to give up. She also couldn't continue to do it alone.

She felt a light kiss on her shoulder, and *that* snapped her back to the present. Hannah pulled herself off him and rolled over until she was able to stand up.

"Mark. I can't do—"

"We weren't doing anything," he said, still lying on her bed.

Kissing my shoulder and pulling me into your arms is not *nothing*. She pulled up her pajama shorts again to cover her nakedness. She'd never been comfortable with her body before and even less now. With the wounds treated, there was no reason for him to be there. So why was he?

"I'm okay. You can go back to whatever you were doing before."

She knew she sounded cold and unappreciative, but the last thing she wanted was to give him the wrong impression. *Or maybe it was the right one, but either way, I don't want him knowing I want him. That will only make it more awkward.*

He got off her bed and stood by her side. "Why were you crying?"

She didn't look up at him. Lying wasn't something that came easily for her. "It hurt. That's all."

Mark stood there for a moment, and she was positive he was going to push the subject. Holding her breath as he moved, she waited for him to pull her into his arms and kiss her. But instead, he brushed past her and left her standing alone. *This is good. This is what I want.*

She grabbed the soiled towel off her bed and threw it

on the floor, then went and laid down, pulling the sheet over her head. *When was I last held in a man's arms? Had it really been years ago? It felt so nice, so . . . safe. Sheltered. Less . . . alone.*

MARK DIDN'T WANT to leave her, and that only angered him. He went into protective mode when he saw the blood. It was all instinct, and he never once had to think about what to do. It was no different than what he would've done for any of his men.

What wasn't natural was his reaction to her. His heart was pounding when she was crying. He could've held her forever and wanted to promise her the world if it'd stop what was hurting her. She might've said it was the alcohol, but he knew that wasn't the only thing.

If she would've opened up to him, he would've been lost. He wasn't sure if he was glad she shut him off or not. *Warm and fuzzy empathy isn't really in my wheelhouse, so I stay far away from such situations. I'd probably be useless anyway.*

When Mark re-entered the second-floor apartment, Don was sitting on the beam waiting.

He wasn't in the mood for any jokes, not even Don's. His emotional state was unexpected. Blood wasn't an issue for him. He'd seen plenty of it and patched up wounds that would make a trauma nurse cringe. So what had shaken him about a small puncture wound? The answer didn't please him. Mark was a man, and everything in him wanted *her*. That was a physical reaction that could easily be explained. That, however, didn't explain why he'd felt a punch in his gut when he felt the blood on his hand or why he felt the need to hold her while she cried.

Mark didn't wear his emotions on his sleeve for people to see, but he knew it would be different with Don. For better or worse neither of them could bullshit the other. He had no choice but to prepare himself for some of Don's harassing, and by the look on his face, it wasn't going to be long before it started.

"Heard some screaming down there. I was almost tempted to see if you needed my help."

And it begins. "Thought you'd have that beam up by now."

"Are you kidding me? You expected me to work while you were downstairs having all the fun?"

"She was hurt. I was just making sure she was okay."

Don laughed. "If I hadn't come in when I did there wouldn't be any work getting done in this place. Don't blame you. She's easy on the eyes and the way she was looking at you . . . Damn. It was like you were one sweet tasty dessert, and she was hungry." *The way she was looking at me?*

Mark normally could laugh at such things but something was different. Hannah wasn't the type of woman to make lewd comments about.

"Leave it alone, Don."

Of course, Don didn't listen. He never did. He enjoyed pushing Mark's buttons, which usually didn't get him very far. It took a lot to get a reaction out of him. Mark knew it was more about what was going on inside him than anything Don was saying. *At least, Hannah isn't around to endure Don's pathetic jokes.*

"And the look on your face when you saw she was bleeding. I wish I'd had a camera. Trust me; you weren't *the controlled* Mark that you always are. Can't believe I was here to witness it."

Neither can I. "Are you planning on talking all morning or can we start this job?"

Don got off the beam and picked up his tool belt. "I can multi-task. Besides, giving you shit will help me forget how fucking hot this place is."

"I warned you about the air conditioner."

"How low on the list is that or can we sneak it up here? Remember, I've been off the job for a few years now."

"Yeah, I can tell; you're out of shape," Mark teased, but Don probably spent half his day working out.

"I seem to remember you complaining about the beam earlier. Maybe you need to hit the gym yourself. But you had no problem swooping Hannah off her feet, did you?"

So close to changing the damn subject. "Give it a rest."

"Hit a nerve, did I?" Don raised his hands as if pushing him wasn't wise. "Easy, Mark. It was an observation. Okay? There's no connection between you and Hannah. It's possible I was wrong." Don mumbled under his breath, "But I wasn't."

Mark wasn't sure if Don had meant for him to hear that last comment or not. Giving him another warning wasn't going to change one damn thing. Don did and said whatever he wanted. He would've been hell to deal with in the military. Honestly, he wouldn't have lasted a day. But as a friend, he made life interesting. If it hadn't been for Don and his sense of humor, he might've snapped after those first few missions. He had a knack for taking a situation and ripping the stress right out of it. *Probably what you're trying to do right now. But stress isn't what I'm feeling. And what I need isn't something he can help me with.*

He might be near Don, but Hannah was first and foremost in his mind. He'd never faced such distraction. If one of his men was in this mindset, he'd tell him to get his head out of his ass and get back to business. There was no room for this in their line of duty. It's what made men get wounded, or worse, killed. He hadn't been there even a week, yet somehow she'd found a way past his defenses. Mark wasn't sure how it happened, but it was the first and hopefully the last time.

It has to be. There can't be anything more than business between us. He bent down and grabbed the sledge hammer. Breaking something sounded great. "Then let's get this job done and get out of here. I have places to be." *Any place other than here. Damn. I'd prefer sleeping on the hot desert sand than alone in my bed just two doors away from hers.*

CHAPTER FIVE

THE REMAINDER OF the day Hannah hid in her bedroom. Partially because she couldn't bring herself to face Mark, and the rest because she never imagined how one small puncture wound could be so painful. Although she wasn't happy when Mark cleaned it, she was grateful it wouldn't get infected. As she got dressed for work, she was regretting she'd agreed to cover the early morning shift. It meant being up at four to get there by five a.m. With little sleep last night, this would've been a perfect day to sleep in.

She grabbed her purse and searched for her keys. Normally she left them in the car so she didn't have to search for them. Since Mark had drilled safety into her head, she found herself doing things she hadn't done since living in Providence with Bailey.

Maybe I should give her a call today. She's wanted to come for a visit. Might as well let her before I lose this place. Besides, I'm totally outnumbered with all this male testosterone suddenly present. Time to even things out a bit.

Hannah opened her bedroom door gently, hoping

not to make any noise. Since she hadn't heard any noise above her, she assumed Mark and Don caught the hint about waiting until daybreak before starting repairs. *Not that I don't want it done, but seven to seven is long enough.*

As she left her room, she couldn't stop herself from turning toward his room. The door was closed. *Good. Stay there till I'm gone. I need to start this day off on a good note, not a lusty one.*

Hannah tiptoed down the hall and exited the house. She saw the lights on in her tenant's apartment as she sat in her car. *Strange. Strange. That man never seems to sleep.* When she first met Jason three months ago, he'd been a sweet, polite young man. She hadn't felt uncomfortable at all. He was attractive, but he didn't affect her like Mark. She'd tried talking to him when he first moved in, but he seemed . . . lost, but not unsettled. That's how she'd felt since her father died, so she didn't push the issue. Giving someone the space they want was sometimes the best thing. Although she was in and out often, she'd only seen him leave the apartment once, and that was very late at night. Hannah wasn't one to judge another only on odd or strange behavior. She thought about the comment Mark made about him. *Should I have done more checks? No. Don't think about it. He pays his rent; that's all you need to be concerned about.*

She started her car and headed to work. There was no point in worrying about it. The possibility of losing the house was fast becoming a reality. She knew there was no way Mark and Don could make the vacant second-floor apartment safe by Friday. There wasn't even a bathroom floor, and the kitchen wasn't much better. *At least Mark and Don will have a place to stay until the bank kicks us all out. I don't know where they'll go afterward, but I'm sure those two will find someone to hire them. Maybe I should write them a letter of recommendation.*

Hannah burst out laughing as she thought to herself what Mark's would say.

To whom it may concern,

I recommend Mark Collins to work shirtless. Also, his butt looks fantastic in jeans. He's great with his hands.

P.S. He also knows first aid.

She had to wipe the tears from her cheeks, picturing his next potential employer reading it. *I'm sure he'd have a line waiting to hire him.*

Then her laughter stopped. She didn't want to think of him working for another woman. That sexy shirtless man was for her enjoyment only. *I never liked sharing as a child, I guess I haven't outgrown it.*

She was almost at the diner when she saw a huge truck pulling away from the hardware store. They didn't normally get large deliveries mid-week. Whatever it was, she was sure the driver had stopped at the diner for breakfast, so she'd soon have the scoop. *One thing about a small town—everyone talks. And that's why I don't want to live in one anymore. Everyone talks but that doesn't mean they have their facts right.*

She remembered the rumor that she'd left home because she was pregnant and didn't want her father to know. Her father had called her to ask if it was true. He was both relieved and crushed to find it wasn't. He'd said he wanted to be a grandpa. Hannah had promised he would be when the time was right. *Yet another promise I couldn't keep, Dad. But neither of us knew how little time you had. I really miss you, Dad. It's not fair. First Mom and then you. Why did you both have to be taken away so young? If only I'd known, I never would've gone away to college. I would've spent every moment here with you making more memories.*

She was tired of counting all the times she'd let him down. The last promise she'd made was about that darn house. Once that one was broken, she'd have nothing left. Closing the door on that would be bittersweet. She would have to live with regret instead of the endless need to make it work, when no matter how hard she tried she was bound to fail.

As she got out of her car, she told herself to put her sweet southern smile on. She'd become a wonderful actress over the past few years. No one could tell if she was faking it or not. *Well, no one except Bailey. Guess that's what a best friend is for.*

Pulling her cell phone out, she debated calling her. She never knew what Bailey was doing. Some nights she did standup comedy, and some days she worked as a certified nursing assistant. The last thing she wanted to do was wake her. So instead she sent a text. *It'll give her time to think of a nice way to tell me no.*

What was it that she wanted to ask? If she sounded desperate, Bailey would be worried, and that wasn't what she wanted. *Really just texting and saying I could use a hug is probably too much. But accurate.*

She put her phone back in her purse. No matter what she texted, Bailey would read right through it.

Just before she entered the diner, her phone dinged. Reaching back in her purse, she pulled it out. *Bailey.*

A smile came across her face as she read the message. One that only a best friend would send.

Miss you. I am boarding a plane today, so you better make up the guest room for me. If you don't let me come this time, you'll never get that pink sweater you let me borrow ten years ago.

She loved Bailey. *I can always count on you to make me laugh.* Hannah didn't need to wait to respond.

Can't wait to see you. So much to tell you, but I'm sure you'll see for yourself when you get here.

Now all she needed was to get through the day at the diner, go home, and clean the house like a mad woman. It wasn't what one would call messy, but the two men coming and going left a trail of dust and dirt on her floors, and their tools were quickly piling up. *Who knows, maybe the maid will clean it while I'm out.*

"MARK, YOU'RE ASKING too much."

"What's the matter? You've been spending so much time behind a camera that you can't handle a field job anymore?"

Don shot him a look. "Look at this bathroom. Who the hell in their right mind runs the electrical wires under the tub and shower? And besides that, the wires aren't even grounded. I'm shocked this place hasn't gone up in smoke."

Mark wasn't going to dispute that. There were more signs of amateur repairs, which he hadn't shown Don. Doing so might cause him to pack up and leave.

"Since we gutted the bathroom, moving the wires shouldn't be an issue."

"Mark, quit trying to make this seem easy."

Quit trying to make it seem impossible. Nothing is impossible if you want it bad enough. His entire career was based on that theory. It kept him and his men alive through some impossible situations.

"The truck is pulling up. You better tell me quickly if we tell the men to bring it in or return it."

Don didn't answer him right away. He stood in the bathroom doorway rubbing his chin, as though he was plotting out each step to calculate the odds of completion. Mark wanted to tell him to hurry the fuck up. Standing there was wasting valuable time. Time was their enemy. Don had expedited the order of a double-wide tub shower, vanity, stove, and refrigerator. This was one of the times it came in handy to have a friend rich as shit. But he also needed him and his genius to get the house up and running.

"Call it, Don. Stay or return," Mark said, his patience wearing thin.

"Keep it. And make sure they bring it all up here and leave it in the living room. Any time we can save right now is going to make a difference. Hope you're up for pulling some twenty-hour days."

Mark smiled and patted Don on the back. "Didn't know there was anything less."

He opened the window and yelled to the men who were standing by the delivery truck. "Bring it in. Bring it up." Then he grabbed his tool belt to get started on ripping out the remaining boards.

"Don, are you sure this is going to fit?"

"That is something you should've thought of before you had me order it."

Don walked over and looked at the box then went back to the bathroom to measure. He was shaking his head. *I'm counting on you right now. Don't give me any bad news, buddy.*

"What's on the other side of this wall?"

"That guy's apartment that you're supposed to be keeping an eye on for me," Mark said softly because he didn't want that bit of information getting out.

"How can I listen when I don't understand a fucking thing he says?"

Mark raised a brow. "What does that mean? If he's talking too quietly, I can get you some equipment to help."

Don shook his head. "Won't help. It's not in English." Before Mark could ask, he raised his hand and said,

"If you want to know what it sounds like, then I suggest we switch rooms. I'll take your guest room with the bed, and you can have my room with the folding cot from like World War II. Really, why was this shit in their house?"

Mark wasn't sure if Don was acting difficult so he could change his accommodations or if there really was something going on that he needed to research. Either way, he needed to find a way to get into that guy's apartment. His gut was saying something was off, but he'd been so distracted with Hannah he'd let a few things slip. That wasn't like him. *And it's not going to happen again.*

"One night, Don. That's all. I'll take your cot."

Don smiled. "Great. And you know the saying if you see it rocking don't com—"

"Shut the fuck up, Don."

Don burst out laughing while grabbing the sledge hammer. "Too easy. Way too fucking easy."

Don was right. When it came to Hannah, he didn't play. That didn't mean what he felt for her was anything more than great concern and empathy for her situation. All he wanted to do was help her and leave. *And that is exactly what I'm going to do.*

But to do this, he needed a way to ensure Hannah didn't see the apartments until they were done and they were heading out. That was going to be far from easy. If he told her not to come upstairs, then she'd be there in a heartbeat just to be defiant. Don was no help; she'd never take anything he said seriously.

I could put locks on the doors and not give her the keys. He knew that'd be a big red flag that he was hiding something. As he picked up the breathing mask, he knew exactly what to say. It wasn't a lie and was a viable reason why she couldn't enter. *This place is filled with mold and asbestos. Both hazardous to your health. There is no way you should enter until we professionals have it all removed.*

"What are you smiling about over there, Mark?"

He looked and Don and said, "I love it when a plan comes together."

"And I love it when you're working while planning. Now get your ass moving already. Or did you forget we are shooting for a miracle here?"

He ignored Don. He was working with an entirely different attitude now. He felt confident that his plan was going to work. And it wasn't even a lie. The place was far from up to code for a rental, but he and Don were going to change that. When they left, she was going to have her feet planted on solid ground. He wouldn't need to worry about her.

Of course, this all was betting on her believing him. If she caught wind that the repair was so much more than what she'd requested, he was sure he'd find out what she meant by her "southern temper."

I can picture your sweet green eyes turning dark with fire. Just like the fiery passion I saw in you when you lay in my arms. Deny it, but we both know it's the truth. Just one problem, I can't and won't give you what you want. Sorry, baby, I know you're hurting, but I hope it makes you feel better to know that you're not suffering alone. And hopefully when I'm gone you'll be stronger and able to move forward.

No amount of cold showers were going to lessen his desire for her. That didn't change the facts though. He was not going to touch her. All he needed to do was keep enough distance between them and in a few weeks when this job was done, she could find someone who could fit into her sweet little home here. *Because a home is not a place I can afford to want. And someone there waiting for me to return would add a stress that'd affect my team.*

I won't let that happen.

They will always come first.

CHAPTER SIX

WHAT HANNAH THOUGHT would be a bad day had turned around quickly. Everything at work went smoothly. She even had one of her biggest tip days yet. Which was good, since what she made was no longer just covering Mark, but Don as well. Feeding two burly men would stretch her more, but she could exist on salads since she still had a garden growing behind her house, Men working as hard as they were needed substantial meals. *Can't let those muscles go to waste. God . . . his muscles.*

If she hadn't blushed thinking about the last time she went to check, she would be looking forward to seeing how much progress they had made. She knew it was a lot of work, but then again Mark spoke as though he had everything under control. Somehow, even though she didn't want to, she took him at his word. Besides there were things she was trying to avoid. *Like seeing Mark shirtless.*

As she pulled into the driveway, she could already hear the power tools. She was glad they were busy. She needed to get things ready for Bailey. She'd stopped at the market on the way home and picked up a few things. Not that she didn't cook for the guys, but the last time she saw Bailey she was on a low-carb, all natural health kick. Granted that was a great way to live, but on such a fixed income, eating healthy wasn't in the picture. *Well, it's going to be for a few days though.*

"You want a hand?"

Mark's deep voice startled her as she was leaning into the door of her car and trying to lift the bags. When she spun around the fresh fruits in the bag she was holding started to tumble to the ground. Mark's reflexes were impressive. He took the bag from her, and like a professional juggler, was able to catch the loose apples as they fell. His hands were moving so quickly her eyes were barely able to keep up. Then he placed them back in the bag before he reached in the back seat of her car and grabbed the rest.

"I'll carry. You get the door." Mark didn't wait for a response and was already halfway up the steps before she even grabbed her purse.

Sure. Thanks. Oh, wait. It wasn't a question, was it? You just take control and forget who the boss is here. Hannah followed him, opened the door, and refused to say one word to him. He put her bags on the kitchen table and stood looking at her. *Look all you want, but I am not going to speak first. Not even to say thank you.*

She started emptying the bags and putting away the items that needed to be refrigerated first. In the heat, it wouldn't take long for groceries to perish. Hannah avoided eye contact with him, hoping he would get the hint and go away. Instead, she saw his feet planted on the same spot with his hands on his hips. *You don't know me if you think I am going to give in.*

There were a few bags on the other side of him. First she tried reaching around him, then decided to go the long way. There was no way she'd say "excuse me" to break the silence. He needed to learn some southern manners and ask, not assume. When you don't ask, you get the cold shoulder. *No matter how handsome you are.*

As she walked around the table and reached for the bag, she heard soft laughter coming from Mark. *You think this is funny? I don't. I have work to do and so do you. Now leave because I'm not getting shit done with you here.*

Hannah continued putting things in the refrigerator. Then the laughter got louder. *Damn you, Mark.* She was no longer looking where she put things, practically throwing them on the shelf.

When she turned to grab something else off the table, she slammed right into him. He'd moved closer to her once again without being heard. *Is he a ninja or something? No one as big as him should be this quiet.*

Hannah didn't step back. She didn't look up. Her hands were by her side as she turned her head as far to the right as she could manage. *I am not budging, Mark. So what's your next move?*

He had one. One that she'd not expected. His hand came up and turned her face to look up at him.

"Is there something you want to say to me?" Mark asked in a serious tone.

A million things. "Yes, there is. It appears you can't afford a shirt. I am willing to purchase one for you if you need me to." She didn't smile, and her tone was dry. If that didn't get him to let go, she wasn't sure what else to try. Threatening him hadn't worked the other day either.

"It's hot." His eyes never left hers as his thumb traced her jaw.

Yes, you're hot. I mean it's hot. Shit. You've got me freaking hot. This is not supposed to be happening. I wanted to make a point and you getting me all hot and wet for you wasn't it. "Mark, please." Instead of the demanding tone she wanted, it was a soft, seductive plead.

He was eager to give her what she apparently was begging him for. His lips claimed hers so tenderly she couldn't stop herself from melting against him. Pulling away and telling him to stop was the farthest thing from her mind. She was tired of fighting this fire that had been building from the moment she first laid eyes on him. *I want him. More than I ever thought I'd want anyone.*

Slipping her arms around his neck, she pulled herself closer to meet his embrace. Hannah felt his body tense as she pressed her body against his. He sucked in a breath. "Hannah." Mark reached down and cupped her bottom, careful to avoid her puncture wound, pulling her up into his arms. Her legs wrapped tightly around his waist. His lips hungrily took hers. Neither held back as they wildly explored each other.

This is the piece of heaven I've been yearning for. I want more, no, I need more. She boldly ran her hands over his broad shoulders, down his biceps, and then back up.

His lips left hers, and she was disappointed until she felt them on her neck, nipping and sucking as he lifted her even higher into his arms.

"You smell sweet," he mumbled against her throat. "Like a meadow of honeysuckle."

Flames of desire shot through her like bolts of lightning. He was all man, rough and tough, yet his touch and words were tender, loving.

"Mark . . ."

He continued kissing her neck and moving downward. "I know." He took one hand from her bottom and cupped her breast through her blouse. He licked from her collarbone to her breast, unbuttoning her shirt as his tongue trailed down her cleavage.

Her nipples were waiting impatiently for him to rip her clothes off and give them the attention they needed. His fingers unfastened the last button, and she arched her back offering herself to him. "I want—"

"Hey Hannah, I'm h—" came Bailey's voice from behind Hannah. "Oh, shit. Sorry."

Shit. Bailey. How did I forget? She tried to pull herself away from Mark. He loosened his grip, so her feet touched the floor, but she was still pressed up against him. She knew why. He was hard and needing her just as much as she needed him.

This is not the time to think about how much either of

us wants or doesn't want each other. My best friend is right behind me, and I want to crawl under the kitchen table and hide.

There was no use. She was going to have to face her. From the look on Mark's face she wasn't leaving.

Stepping back slightly, she turned, forcing a smile. She knew her cheeks were burning and not only from embarrassment, but from the passion waiting to be released. *Holy shit that man can kiss. I want more. . . Deep breath, Hannah. Your company has arrived.*

"How about some introductions?" Bailey asked.

Hannah pointed to Mark and said, "He's um . . ."

"Mark," he stated.

She looked up at him. *If you only knew how many times I call your name out in my sleep.* She shook her head as though the memory of his kisses could be erased so easily.

Then Hannah turned to her friend. "This is . . ." She was so flustered that she became tongue-tied.

"I'm Bailey Tasca. Hannah's best friend; the same friend she asked to come and stay here because she was lonely." Bailey laughed. "Maybe autocorrect changed your text from horny to lonely? Because lonely is not how I'd describe you right now."

I'm so going to kill you when we're alone, Bailey.

"I should probably get back to work," Mark said as he released her.

Instantly she was lonely for his arms on her again. Yet she also wanted to see Bailey so much. *Timing really sucked.*

"Work?" Bailey looked at Mark then back to Hannah.

"Yes, he's here working on the place."

"Oh. Work. Yeah. I could so tell." Bailey laughed softly again.

Hannah gave her a warning look before turning to Mark. "Sorry, but it looks like you'll need to bunk with Don for a few days while Bailey is here."

"Don?" Bailey asked.

"A friend working here as well," Mark answered her.

"Does he look anything like you?" Bailey winked at Mark.

"They are here to *work*," Hannah said firmly.

"Thanks for the invite, Hannah. I think I'm going to enjoy this visit even more than I first thought."

Hannah was still rolling her eyes as Mark headed toward the guest room.

"Will you stop it already? You're embarrassing him," Hannah said to Bailey in the sternest voice she could muster.

"Mark doesn't seem fazed at all. Or should I say not embarrassed at all." She was grinning and looking in the direction Mark had walked.

Oh, please save me from all this. Why couldn't it have been Don who caught us? Or better yet, why did we have to get caught at all? Is one night of sweet hot passionate sex too much to ask for? Looking at her friend, she knew the answer. *At least I know we'll have a good laugh over this once we are alone.*

Mark came back down the hall a minute later, carrying his bag. "I had actually come by to let you know you can't enter the vacant apartments until we give you the go ahead. It's full of mold and asbestos. Both are hazardous, and I don't want you getting sick." Then he turned back to Bailey. "That goes for you as well. You both are confined to this apartment or the grounds outside."

"Excuse me? Are you telling me where I can go in my own house?" Hannah seemed indignant at his outrageous request and faced him with her hands on her hips.

He looked her squarely in the eyes and said, "Absolutely."

She was still huffing at the audacity of him speaking to her like that. When he was gone she turned to Bailey and said, "I can't believe that, can you?"

"I know, right? That man is hotter than hell, and he likes you too. How did you get so lucky?"

Lucky? I don't feel lucky. I feel as if too many things are against me. But thinking about who had just been pressed against her, she could admit Bailey was also right. *That. Man. Is. Hot.*

MARK CARRIED HIS duffle back into the apartment across from Hannah's. Don came down from the apartment he was working on upstairs at the same time.

"Where the hell have you been? I thought you were supposed to get us something cold to drink and get back to work?"

He turned and looked at Don. "Something came up." *And damn it, I need a cold shower more than I need work. I also need to scrub from my mind how amazing Hannah felt in my arms. How she pressed herself into my arms as if it was the most natural thing in the world. And then she forget her best friend's name. That was priceless. And that's just with a kiss. Imagine if we weren't interrupted. Fuck. It would've been mined blowing.*

As Mark put his bag on the floor, Don laughed. "I can't believe you're actually going to give me the guest room and you take my cot."

"Don't believe it because it's not happening."

He looked at Mark then said, "You and Hannah have a fight, and she kicked you out?"

"Let me say this again. There is nothing between Hannah and me. And no she didn't kick me out. She has company, and they need privacy. That's all." *If she knew she had a friend coming, why did she put me in her spare room for the first few nights? Did she want me close? Was she hoping for more than just a renovation on the house? Because if that was the case . . .* He shook off that thought. It didn't matter what she wanted, because the way she looked at him was only going to come with entanglements he wasn't interested in.

"What's her company's name?"

"Bailey."

Don shook his head. "Are you going to let some guy come in and snag the sweetest thing you've ever laid your eyes on? That is not the Mark I know. He never walks away from something he wants. Like having my ass sweating upstairs when it could be on a beach somewhere."

He was right. Mark never walked away from anything once his mind was set. But all he promised himself he'd do was save this family homestead. He was going to uphold that. But that was as far as his connection was going. He'd never intended to kiss her, but she was a little spitfire and the way she challenged him with her eyes drove him crazy. One minute he wanted to know why she was so angry at him for helping her and the next she was offering herself to him. If her friend hadn't interrupted, he would've tasted every sweet inch of her. But instead, he was stuck bunking with Don.

"Bailey is a woman."

Don arched a brow. "Tell me more."

"Sure. Let's talk about it upstairs where work is waiting for us."

Don didn't move. "Wait one minute. You want me to go back upstairs where it feels like we're working in a sauna when there might be a beautiful woman waiting to meet someone with my charm just across the hall?"

"This is not a vacation, Don."

"It was when you called me."

Don knew that wasn't going to be the case right from the beginning. Mark didn't take vacations. He never relaxed. The best he hoped for was to stop thinking of the last mission long enough to find some peace. That wasn't something Don would understand. It didn't mean he didn't try, but his way of showing support was asking him to a bar or club. Mark didn't want crowds or noise. He truthfully was seeking solitude. He was getting neither here.

"I told her neither of them could go anywhere but her apartment and outside. This should ensure we have no unexpected guests."

"Don't pretend you weren't enjoying her little visit. Hell, you got to play hero and even better, doctor."

"You can be a real ass sometimes."

"No extra charge."

"If you're done let's get back—"

Mark didn't finish as something caught his attention. A voice he'd not heard before but yelling briefly in a dialect, unfortunately, he understood. It stopped as quickly as it'd started. *Damn. I need to know who is living up there. Who the fuck is he? And why the fuck is he here? At Hannah's house? No one comes and lives out here so far away from everything for no reason, and I'm going to figure out his.*

This is not only about Hannah any longer.

Don hadn't questioned him. He'd known him long enough to know when he was dead serious, and this was one of those times. Once it was silent up above again, he updated Don with what he could.

"I need you to go and take care of getting the bathroom framed."

"I know that look, Mark. What's going on? What did you hear?"

He didn't want to speak too quickly. Currently, it was only his gut talking, nothing more. For Mark, that was enough, but for anyone else it wouldn't be.

"I'm not sure, Don. But I need to do some research. Just finish up the framing, and I'll be up shortly to help drop the tub into place."

"Great. That means by the end of the day we should be ready to paint and tomorrow put in the linoleum and set the toilet and vanities."

"We should be able to get it all done before we go to bed."

Don shook his head. "Great, another night of no sleep."

He didn't put up any argument. Don was a man who would go the extra mile with Mark, and he knew it. No matter what it took, Don was going to see this through. *That's why I called him.* It was surprising in some respects. In the Navy, his men knew to comply with his demands because that was their job, and he had earned their respect. Don was his own man, with his own typically selfish agendas and lifestyle that he happily enjoyed. Yet he came. *And he won't leave until we are both done. How I earned such a good friend is beyond me, but right now I'm thankful as fuck for the crazy idiot he is. I better make sure the next vacation I invite him to has more of a view than four walls and power tools.*

"Just remember who's doing all the work up there while you do whatever it is you need to do."

"Appreciate it, Don."

Mark was already digging through his duffle bag as Don left the room. He'd hidden his weapon deep inside to go unnoticed. There might not be any reason for it now, but better safe than sorry. He stuck the M1911 inside the back of his jeans. Then he pulled out a T-shirt and put it on. *I know you'd be disappointed, Hannah, but right now I need to conceal something, and it's not my body.*

He knew she was enjoying the view. He'd caught her so many times checking him out. It wasn't that he hadn't done his share of the same to her, but he was better at concealing it. She had one sweet-looking ass, and when she leaned over the car door his cock had sprung to attention. He hadn't lost control over physical reactions since he was a teenager. But when he was around Hannah, something snapped and a want like he'd never experienced before took over. Most people would love it, but Mark hated it. Anything he couldn't control was an issue. Especially with what he had just heard. "Transactions processed non-traceable. Awaiting further instructions."

Mark couldn't act on that. He needed to know exactly who and what he was dealing with. It's not like he could go to Hannah and say, "Kick your tenant out because I have suspicions." And if something was going on, he didn't want the guy catching wind that someone was onto him. If he took off, he'd only set up shop someplace else, and who knows if anyone would get so damn lucky as to stumble across him again. Nope, this was on him for now. Once he had anything solid, he would reach out to Lionel Johnson to rally the team, but he still had them hanging close to Casey and Derrick without their knowledge, just in case things went sour there. *I might need to think about expanding my team if I'm pulling all this off-duty security work. Then again, the people we are protecting have no clue we're even doing it. And it's better that way.*

He sat on the floor, closed his eyes, quieted his breathing, and listened closely. He needed to concentrate on every sound. Then slowly eliminate them. First to go were the sounds of Don and his tools, then the sound of Hannah's sweet laughter that echoed through him. It's a sound he would never grow tired of hearing. But it was a distraction now. *Focus. Think of what could be at stake. Think of your country.*

Within seconds everything was drowned out except the voice he wanted to hear. It was faint and only speaking periodically, but what he said wasn't anything significant. It was more of a one-way conversation, and the guy upstairs was doing all the listening.

That's not going to give me any information. I need to see this guy. Talk to him. He stood and headed to Don. *I need to get in that apartment.*

When Mark entered the apartment, Don was doing the finishing touches on the framing. "Mark, you're just in time. The final nail is going in, and then we're ready to set the tub and shower." Don finished hammering it in. "I think I am going to take a long soak in this tub tonight. I know you're not tired from all the research, but someone's been busting his ass up here in the hundred-degree temperatures."

Mark stood staring at the wall. Don did great work and accomplished more than anyone else could have.

"Go ahead. Tell me it looks great. I think there is more room in my ego."

"Looks sturdy."

"Well, of course it is. Nothing is taking this thing down. I have reinforced the studs. The whole house might fall, but this wall isn't going anywhere."

That was exactly what he'd expected from Don. Anything less would've been disappointing. But he didn't care about the wall or the tub. All he cared about was getting into the apartment next door. Hannah had said he never lets anyone inside and never comes out. So many red flags jumped out at him, like how does he get cash to pay the rent each month and how does he get his food if he's not leaving. *What am I missing?* He knew there was something, but he couldn't figure it out. He needed a visual inside. *How am I going to get in without getting approval from Hannah? She'll need to give him forty-eight hours notice. If there is anything to see, it'll be long gone. I need a reason to get in.*

He looked at his watch. 23:00 This was when the guy seemed to be the most active. Sneaking in was going to be difficult, most would say impossible. *I've never allowed impossible in my vocabulary before, and I'm not going to now.*

He needed to think. There was a way, he'd just not

seen it yet.

"Serious, Mark. Feel this wall. I mean the guy on the other side won't even hear the water running with this. It's almost soundproof."

Exactly. He won't hear anything.

Mark stepped out of the bathroom, went to where all the tools were stored, and found the sledge hammer. *Sorry, Don. There's no other way.*

When he entered again, Don said, "Mark, trust me, it's perfect. And any finishing work will require a much smaller tool.

Mark walked past Don and stood in front of the wall. *Some things are more important than the deadline.*

Gripping the sledge hammer tightly he swung it over his shoulder and with full force let it come crashing down on the first stud.

"What the hell are you doing? Have you lost your fucking mind?"

Mark swung again and heard the board snap. Then a third and fourth swing. The wall was not only giving, but he knew he was breaking through to the other side. He had no idea what the setup was like. Usually a house had all the plumbing adjacent to each other, but nothing had been normal in this house. They'd never heard running water as they were working in the bathroom, so he could eliminate it being a bathroom or kitchen. For all he knew he was knocking into a closet or bedroom. Either was fine with him as long it meant he was getting in that apartment.

He didn't want to make it too obvious, so when it was cracked just enough, Mark hit the new PVC piping which caused the water to start shooting out.

"Mark, you've lost your mind."

Mark reached for the pipe and pointed it in the direction to blow water into the next apartment. Then he turned to Don and said, "When you hear me say pipe wrench, I want you to turn off the shut-off value. Don't touch anything until you hear me say pipe wrench. Understood?"

He started leaving the room, and Don started to follow. "Stay here. I don't know who is in that apartment."

"Exactly, Mark. I've got your back."

"This isn't a fight, Don. This is research."

"I wish you could've done it before I spent six hours creating perfection."

Mark bolted out of the apartment and banged on the tenant's door. "Hey, we broke a pipe. I need to get in or your apartment is going to flood. Come on. Open up or your place is going to flood."

The door opened, and a young man in his midtwenties asked, "Who are you?"

Mark pushed past him. "The repairman. And right now it's your place that needs fixing."

"I don't want anyone in here."

"Come with me and you'll see. Your apartment is going to flood."

Mark's eyes scanned every inch of the apartment as he made his way to the side where he knew he'd broken through. The kid was right behind him and looked nervous as shit.

"Look." Mark pointed at the water coming through the hole in the wall.

"What happened?"

"My partner slipped with the hammer and smashed right through the wall." Mark dropped to his knees and reached into the hole that he'd made only moments before.

"You have no right to come into my house. You need to leave."

"One more minute and I'll have it off. If only I had a pipe wrench, this would be so much easier."

The water slowed then stopped.

"There. No more water."

"Now you leave."

"You don't want me to stay and clean up the water and patch the wall from your side?"

The guy shook his head. "I'll do it. Now go. I need my rest."

Good try. I already know you don't sleep at night. "Sorry. I didn't mean to wake you. I'll make sure he's more careful in the future."

The guy followed closely, as they walked to the door. He said nothing as he closed the door tightly. Mark heard the door being bolted behind him.

If I need to come back, that won't stop me.

He entered the apartment where Don was standing, looking not too happy. He couldn't blame him. This was not anything he signed up for. *Being my friend isn't always easy.*

"Care to explain?"

Mark said, "Downstairs."

Neither spoke until they were behind closed doors and Mark was comfortable no one could hear. Not the man upstairs or the lovely Hannah.

"We have an issue here."

"I figured that when you decided to destroy the place. What exactly is the issue?"

Even though he'd trust Don with his life, this was not about him. It had the potential to be government business.

"The guy was suspicious as hell. I needed to do more digging."

"So I should stop the repairs? This is not the most efficient way to remodel a home."

Don's sarcasm was appreciated. He needed to keep it light between them. No one needed to know what he suspected. *Only if there is something they need to know, will I bring them into the loop.*

"I won't break down any more walls without talking to you first."

"Great, but if you do, next time why don't you take the blame? I can't believe you threw me under the bus like that. Should I expect everything that goes wrong to be my fault from here on in?"

Mark laughed. "Yeah, pretty much."

"Thanks for the advance warning. I won't try so hard

to impress anyone if I'm going to be the fuck-up."

"No one here for you to impress Don." Mark gave him a warning look.

"Point taken. But I'm telling you, next vacation spot I'm picking, and you're not going to have any say in it at all."

"We'll see about that." Mark was in the habit of giving orders, not taking them unless they came in an official document.

"Not going to tell me what you saw?"

"Just keep your eyes and ears open and your mouth shut. I don't want Hannah or her friend catching wind that I'm—"

"Researching. Yeah, I know."

Mark nodded and pulled out his cell phone. "You might as well get some sleep. Tomorrow's going to be a long day."

And I have some digging to do, and it's best you're not looking over my shoulder while I do it.

CHAPTER SEVEN

"**B**AILEY, I CAN'T believe you!"

She smiled and asked, "What? You mean standing there, watching you kiss some hunk in your kitchen?" Bailey grabbed a drink from the fridge and took a seat at the kitchen table as if she, too, had grown up in that house. Hannah saw her friend's bags sitting in the foyer. As always, Bailey had packed like she was moving in permanently.

"Yes, that too."

"Well, that's what you get for inviting me over and not sharing that you have a hottie of a boyfriend. Or was this your way of telling me?"

He is a hottie, isn't he? Hannah shook the thought from her mind. "He isn't my anything. He works for me, but besides that, he's nothing to me," Hannah said with her hands on her hips as though that was going to help get her point across.

"So are you lying to just yourself or me too? Because, what I saw was no professional relationship. You are so into that guy. And just in case you haven't noticed, he's into you as well."

I don't want to think about it. It's an impossible situation. One that will only end in having my heart broken.

"You're reading too much into it. It was just a kiss."

Bailey raised a brow, not buying a word of it. "Hannah, you were in the man's arms and if I hadn't entered, I'm sure there would have been a lot more than just some heavy petting going on. Damn. I was jealous. I can't even remember the last time a man held me like that."

"Will you please drop the subject?" Her voice was sharper than she intended.

Bailey patted the seat next to her. "We've been friends for ten years. You and I have discussed everything with each other. All the good times and all the bad. I am not going to let you shut me out now."

She was right. Their friendship meant everything to her. Hannah took the seat next to her but didn't know what to say. "It is all very confusing."

"Anything with men usually is."

Bailey had so much more experience with men than she did. All Hannah had was a boyfriend in high school who she kissed a few times and one guy she dated for the year she was in Providence. *Maybe talking it out with Bailey will help me get my head on straight. Understand what I'm feeling.*

"Okay, but please don't make fun of me."

"Hannah, I'm your friend; of course, I'm going to tease you about it. But only because I love you, and you know that."

Oh, I do. I don't know how I could've gotten through these past few years without her. If she hadn't come when my dad died, I think I would've lost my mind.

"So why don't you start by telling me where you met Mark."

Hannah hesitated. She couldn't claim they had the most romantic of meetings. "Have I told you about my cousin Sissie in Texas?"

Bailey rolled her eyes. "The one who owns the bar that you'd go visit during the summer when you were a kid?"

"Yep, the one and only. I guess Mark was there visiting his sister or something when Sissie met him. Apparently, they got to know each other. He said he was a contractor. She gave him my number, he accepted the job, and bingo, now he's here."

Bailey was tapping her fingers on the table and shaking her head in disbelief. "What kind of contractor? For all you know Sissie was drunk and doesn't even remember giving him your number. You know how she gets."

"I don't know. The kind that fixes houses obviously. Sissie wasn't drunk, and you know good and well just because she runs a bar doesn't mean she's a drunk. Heck, I'm not sure I've ever seen her drink a lick of alcohol in all the years I stayed with her. She is loud and wild already. You don't want to add alcohol to enhance that personality." Hannah laughed softly. It was then she realized how much she missed seeing Sissie too. "Wow, it's been too long since I've seen her. Yet she is still watching out for her baby cousin."

"You're right. I shouldn't have said that about your cousin. But I've heard the stories and I do want to meet her someday."

"Maybe someday you will."

"Let's get back to business. I want to make sure I understand clearly. You're telling me you let this man in your house, and you don't have any references or know exactly what he does? He could be a—"

"He's not." Hannah couldn't believe she was getting the same lecture from her best friend that she received from Mark the first day they met. *Why is everyone worried that some creep is out to get me? I'm a grown woman.*

"What's his last name?"

"Collins. Why?"

"Where is he from?"

Hannah struggled to remember if he ever mentioned that. "I don't know."

"What company does he work for?"

And this is where it gets awkward. She's really going to question my sanity now. "He doesn't have a job."

"You said he's a contractor."

She shrugged her shoulders. "That's what Sissie told me, and I trust her, Bailey. I didn't have a mother growing up, but she was the closest thing I had. She's atypical, but I know she loves me and wouldn't send anyone who would hurt me."

"Oh, Hannah. What am I going to do with you?" She pulled out her cell phone. "Okay, first let me see what I can find about Mark Collins. You said he has family in Texas. I'm going to guess in Honeywell where Sissie lives."

She sat while Bailey tried a few Google searches. "Bailey, I don't feel comfortable with you doing this."

"Why?" Bailey looked at her as if she had two heads.

"I guess I don't want anyone snooping on me, so I don't snoop on them."

"Oh, that's sweet. Very naïve, and you might end up a victim of a horrible crime, but very sweet."

Bailey searched some more but appeared to find nothing.

"He doesn't seem to be flagged as a serial killer or anything, so stop worrying. He's not on the most wanted list, sexual or criminal." She put her phone away. "My psychopath radar didn't go off when I met him, so I'll give him the benefit of the doubt, but I need more information. You said he isn't working, so how is he here? Or better yet why is he here?"

"That is simple. He needs a place to stay, and I need help."

"You mean he's homeless?"

"Yes."

"So there are two old vehicles parked outside. I take it they belong to Mark and his friend?"

Oh, this is going to be a long night at this rate. "Yes. Let me save you some time by telling you everything I know."

"Finally!"

"He travels from place to place and works very cheap. I mean honestly, Bailey, I'm paying him so you know he isn't charging much. When he saw how big the job was, he reached out to his friend, Don, who is also really struggling. This works out great for everybody concerned. I will get my house repaired, and they aren't sleeping under a bridge somewhere."

"Hannah. I need you to be really honest with yourself here. When you look at Mark, do you see that man jobless, never mind homeless? No way. He's built like he spends half his day in a gym. Something about this doesn't feel right. Homeless? Jobless? Totally broke? I know, don't judge him, but someone has to keep their feet planted on the ground and not wrapped around the waist of some beefcake." Bailey waved her hand in front of her face like a fan. "Damn, girlfriend, that was a hot scene I walked in on."

She didn't want to think about it. "Well, that was a one-time thing. It's never going to happen again." *It can't happen again. She's right. I don't know him well enough. Hell, I don't know him at all. I only know how he makes me feel when he's close—amazing and scary as hell. But it doesn't matter anymore as it's not happening again. Never again.*

Hannah knew she'd need to tell herself that over and over because she didn't believe it either. His kisses were like chocolate melting in her mouth. All they did was leave her wanting more.

Stop thinking about it. "I'm really glad you could

come for a visit. I've missed you so much."

"Even with Mark here?"

Especially with him here. "You're my BFF."

Bailey hugged her and said, "You know it, girl. Now let's talk about something else."

"Sounds good. It's been too long since we've seen each other."

"I know. The last time I was here was when your dad passed away."

Hannah couldn't get that time out of her mind. So many people from the area had come to pay their respects, but Bailey... she'd come all the way from Rhode Island just to make sure she was okay. *Always a faithful and dear friend.*

"Yeah, and things haven't gotten any easier since then either."

"Why? You don't have to stay here, you know. You can go back to Providence with me. I have an extra bedroom with your name on it anytime you want it."

She knew Bailey was sincere with her offer. "I truly want to, but I can't."

"Mark?"

I wish it was that simple. "No. My father's last coherent conversation with me was about this house. He asked, no begged, me to keep this place and raise my family here one day."

Bailey looked at her with concern. "Is that what you want? I know years ago you said you wanted out of here. That you'd never return, but it's okay if you changed your mind. That's a perk of being a woman. You had five years in and were only three years off finishing vet school, hon. Your dad's not here anymore. He wouldn't' know or care if you had to sell and move away. I'm sure all he would want is for you to be happy. Are you happy, Hannah?"

Hannah wasn't sure what she wanted. That was one of the major problems. One minute she wanted to be here and then next she wished to be as far away as she could get. *Why isn't it clearer what I should do?*

"Hannah, you don't have to decide right away. Remember my door is always open to you."

"Thank you, Bailey. One day I might take you up on that."

"Enough serious talk."

"Agreed." Hannah didn't ask Bailey down for a visit so they could get all sad and emotional.

"Let's start by you telling me how he kissed. Because when I came in your legs had a death grip around his waist, you were moaning your head off, and your clothes were still on."

Hannah laughed and shook her head. *If she thought that was hot, she should've felt that impressive, hot, hard cock pressed against my core, but we're so not going there. Yes, this is going to be a long, fun night. Somehow Bailey always knows how to make me smile, even when I don't know I need cheering up. I'm so thankful for that.*

Chapter Eight

"MARK. MARK!" HANNAH screamed up the stairs. *He said I couldn't go up there, but the least he can do is answer me when I call for him.*

"I don't mind running up there to get him for you," Bailey offered sweetly.

"Dangerous for me is also dangerous for you."

"Do you really believe it's dangerous? He's probably just sitting up there watching television or something and doesn't want to get caught screwing off."

Bailey had a point. Hannah honestly had no idea what they were doing upstairs; that's why she was yelling for him. Before the construction started, her apartment needed work, but not a renovation. Last night it sounded like they were having a wild frat party and the guys were wrestling or something.

She had warned him about working so early in the morning, but was she going to need to do the same for the middle of the night? Although she and Bailey were still talking hours after the commotion upstairs stopped, that wasn't the point. How was he to know they were awake until the wee hours of the morning reminiscing about the good ole college days?

This morning she was dragging, totally exhausted, and all she wanted was a slow, peaceful start to her day. That changed the moment she walked into her bathroom and found her ceiling was wet and water was on the floor.

Standing at the bottom of the staircase, she called out one last time, "Mark." If he didn't respond, she was going to march upstairs no matter what he said.

It wasn't Mark who appeared but his friend, Don.

"Morning, Hannah. Mark stepped out for a minute. Can I be of some help?"

He was speaking to her, but she saw his eyes on Bailey. Who wouldn't look at her? She was perfect. Tall, dark hair, with an athlete's body. Total opposite of her.

Bailey was playing right along too. "You must be Don."

Don reached his hand to Bailey. Hannah thought a quick handshake and they could get back to the issue at hand, the ceiling in her bathroom. But instead, Bailey reached out her hand and Don brought it to his lips and kissed it.

Bailey acted all sweet and shy, and Don was eating it up. Hannah rolled her eyes. Their little flirting session was not the reason she was standing there. Neither of them seemed to remember she was in the hallway with them.

"And you must be the lovely Bailey."

"Bailey, this is Don Farrell. Don, this is Bailey Tasca. Now can we talk about what *I* need for a minute?" Hannah was shocked at how snappy she sounded. She wasn't sure why. *So what? A man I don't even care about is flirting with my friend. I'm not jealous.*

As she looked at her friend's face then back at Don, it dawned on her. *I am jealous. I want this. I want the fun and easy flirting to be Mark and me. But there can't be any us. It's not meant to be. I know it, and I think he does too. But I don't want a reminder of what I'm missing.*

Don finally let go of Bailey's hand and said to Hannah, "Sorry. I was lost in her sweet green eyes."

Hannah wanted to remind Don that she had green eyes too, but the man was captivated with Bailey. Hannah was used to that. She had the outgoing, bubbly personality that drew people to her. She found the saying that blondes have more fun was so overrated. Bailey was fierce and fearless. *And here I am pretending to be both, when the truth is I'm a marshmallow and ruled by fear. I'm just really good at not letting people see it.*

"That's nice, but it won't fix my wet bathroom, will it?"

Don arched his brow then his eyes widened. "You have water in your bathroom?"

She nodded and waved for him to follow her so she could show him. They'd just entered her apartment when a loud crash rumbled through it. "What the—?"

As she tried to run to the noise, Don grabbed her arm and said, "Wait here."

She had no intention of staying put and started to follow. Then another hand reached out and grabbed her arm. Turning, she saw Bailey's hand holding her arm.

"He said to wait."

Bailey had never been a rule follower. Heck, anytime Hannah got in trouble in college it was because Bailey had talked her into doing something she swore they'd never get caught for. The worse time was when they were caught in their bikinis, swimming in the school pool after it closed. The school took pictures of them swimming and then posted pictures of them cleaning the girls' locker room in their bathing suits as a warning that crime does not pay. It wouldn't have been so bad except that photo also made the local newspaper as an example of how serious the college was in cutting down partying. Hannah never drank alcohol, but from that day forward people would approach her with cards saying who she could call if she needed a designated driver.

"This is my house, Bailey. I need to know what is going on."

"I agree, but what can you do about it?"

Hannah looked at her then down the hall to where Don had run off to. There was nothing she could do. She'd proven that over and over again these last few years. *No matter how hard I try, I have no control over anything. Not my dad's illness and not this house falling down around me. Why do I allow myself to hope? Hope is for fools who believe it will happen. I know and live in reality. It's not pretty, but it's mine. No matter how I try, and how much time these two guys are willing to give me, I can't pull off the impossible. Miracles are for other people. They don't happen to me.*

Don came back out of the bathroom, and the look on his face spoke volumes. *Maybe I don't want to know what happened.*

"Hope you ladies don't need anything important in there."

"Why?" She closed her eyes as though the answer would be less painful doing so.

"A pipe broke last night. I guess more water got out than we thought."

"I can deal with water."

"It caused your entire horsehair plastered ceiling to come crashing down. Surprisingly your shut-off valve was working so I was able to stop your entire apartment from being flooded."

There wasn't that much water. What is he talking about? My entire apartment? "I could've soaked up the water with a towel."

"That may have been the case before the ceiling smashed your toilet and water was gushing everywhere. Or don't you notice I'm a bit wetter than before I went in?"

Hannah looked at him and only then noticed his pants were soaking wet. *No toilet. And this has to happen when I have company? Why? Is there any other way besides the hard way?*

"How did this happen? I mean the water from upstairs in the first place?" If it was their fault, then no matter how bad she felt that they had no place to go, they were both out of there today. She might want to help them, and but she couldn't afford any more repairs than she already had. *Actually, I can't afford any repairs never mind more.*

"Old houses. Things let go. We were lucky last night that Mark just happened along when the pipe broke. Otherwise, you'd be looking at much more damage than just one room down here."

Old rundown houses like this, you mean. Dad, why hadn't you told me how bad things were here? You didn't need to be sending me money at college when you needed it to take care of things at home. Maybe if you had, things wouldn't be the way they are now.

Tears started streaming down her face.

"Look at what you did. You made her cry," Bailey said to Don.

"What did I say?" Don asked puzzled.

Hannah just stood there, her face in her hands, crying and trying to block everyone out.

"What the hell is going on here?" Mark barked from behind her and Bailey.

"Your friend made Hannah cry!" Bailey shot at Mark. "And she doesn't cry. She's one of the toughest people I know. I didn't see her cry when her dad died, so whatever he said, must have really hurt."

Mark shot Don a questioning look.

"I didn't say anything, trust me," Don said seriously.

"Everyone out," Mark said.

"I'm not leaving my friend," Bailey said, wrapping her arms around Hannah's shoulders. "As you can see, she needs me right now."

Don gently touched Baileys' arm. "Let's give them some privacy. If she doesn't want Mark around, I'm sure she'll let us know."

Bailey said firmly, "I'll be on the porch if you need me, Hannah." Then more softly Hannah heard her say to Mark, "If you hurt my friend, you'll answer to me."

Hannah heard them arguing and wanted it to stop, but she couldn't bring herself to speak. All she felt was weakness within her, and she didn't want anyone to witness it. The room became quiet, and she hoped they'd all gone.

But she wasn't alone. The strong arms she'd come to know were being wrapped around her. She didn't need to open her eyes. It was Mark's touch. One she yearned for. Like he had when he'd held her on the bed, he simply held her, tenderly, and let her cry it all out. It didn't matter if the others were there or not. Mark was there and holding her. For the first time in ages, she didn't feel alone. Everything didn't feel so overwhelming anymore. It was like the weight on her shoulders was lifted.

She sniffled as the tears stopped. Hannah didn't want him to let go. She felt safe, secure, and she didn't want that feeling to end. But he did let go. His arms slowly loosened around her, and she knew she'd be facing the issues at hand once again, alone.

But he didn't leave. Instead, he reached for her hand, led her to the living room, and had her sit on the couch. He left the room, but she heard the faucet in the kitchen running, and he came back with a cold glass of water. *Damn you, Mark. Why are you being so sweet?*

MARK HATED SEEING her cry, but hearing that Don was the cause shook him up more than he could justify to himself. *Why? I've seen more women cry in my lifetime than I can count. So why is this one affecting me so much? She's not hurt, not dying, so why do her tears feel like they are physically squeezing my heart?*

All he knew was she was upset, and he needed to be there. Not Bailey, but him. She might not want him there, but he didn't care. As long as he was there, she was under his wing, his protection, and she was just going to need to deal with it.

He sat down beside her and waited until she drank some of the water before he spoke. "Hannah. Bailey said Don made you cry. Tell me what happened. Tell me what he said."

Mark wasn't sure if Don had let it slip about what went down last night. He normally was one he could trust, but there was so much he'd left out that it was possible Don hadn't taken it as seriously as he should've.

"It's too hard to explain."

"Why don't you give it a try?"

She looked at him, her sweet green eyes still glistening from the tears. He wanted to kiss them away. Tell her that he was here and nothing would ever hurt her again. But the truth was, he was here now, and that was all he had to offer her. *Sad, but true. Even if I wanted to be the man for her, I couldn't be. I'd be gone so much and she'd cry for a whole other reason.*

He'd seen so many marriages end or suffer tremendous strain due to the husband's or wife's deployment. And the ones still married, they missed their kids' birthdays, graduations, and hell one even missed his daughter's wedding. They'd received the message about it, but they were so deep undercover on a mission they'd been working on for nine months that they couldn't let him go. Oh, he could've gone but not without jeopardizing the mission and the other men. And when it came to the team, the mission and each other came first. It was how they survived out there. If something went wrong, all they had was each other. Help would come, but there was no guarantee it was going to make it in time.

"Mark, you're not here to listen to my problems."

"I'm here for many reasons, Hannah. So tell me."

"This place is getting to me that's all."

He understood why. There was so much to do and no one there for her. All he could picture was what it would've been like for Casey if she had to face things all alone. Things might have ended so differently for her. Hannah didn't have a big brother watching out for her, never mind any parents. He was glad she had Bailey, who stuck up for her, but she was only here for a short visit.

"Is it the amount of work?"

Hannah laughed, but he knew it wasn't genuine. "You think? I mean every time I turn around you are telling me more bad news."

"What did Don tell you?"

"He told me about the old pipe that broke last night."

Good job. Not true, but believable.

"We got that fixed quickly."

"Obviously, not quick enough."

"Why?"

"You don't know?"

I know more than you think, but not about whatever it is you know. Mark shook his head. "No."

"The water last night started leaking through my bathroom ceiling, and we didn't know until this morning."

Shit, I should've thought about that before I decided to break that pipe. "We can fix that easily. Give us an hour and you'll never notice a thing."

"You might want to take a look in there yourself before you talk anymore."

Mark knew a gallon of paint, and it would be even better than before. But the expression on her face said he better do as she said. Getting up from the couch, he walked to the bathroom. The door normally opened to the inside, but when he turned the knob and pushed, it only went a quarter of the way. He stuck his head inside to see what was blocking it. *What the fuck!?* The entire ceiling was on the floor, and he could also see the porcelain toilet broken in two. *This entire fiasco was my doing. I'm trying to make her life better. Instead, I ruin the only nice bathroom in the place. And worse, when she has a friend visiting. Damn. I understand why Don blamed it on old plumbing just giving way. It was better than the truth; this was no accident. But now she hates this place when she really should hate me.*

Mark closed the door and went back to Hannah.

"Is it as bad as Don made it out to be?"

Hasn't she even seen it yet? Damn, Don. You're not making this any easier on me, buddy. Nodding, Mark said, "Most likely worse. Don's a good guy, and he doesn't like to hurt anyone."

Hannah met his eyes as she asked, "Unlike you?"

"Unlike me." *So unlike me. Don was likeable. I was someone men followed and that was about it. And Hannah can see clearly the difference.* Still, he didn't like the sorrow in her eyes, and he needed to fix that.

He got up and said before he left, "Don and I can fix that real cheap. Your bathroom will look even better when we're done. But for now, it looks like you ladies will need to share ours across the hall."

"That one is disgusting and barely works."

"Which is a step above yours. I can build you an outhouse if you'd rather, but the options are very limited at the moment."

She was quiet for a minute as though weighing her options. "Okay, but I have one request."

He'd give her the world if she asked. "What is it?"

"We ladies would appreciate it very much if you please put the toilet seat down when you're done."

Sweet Hannah. You won't let life keep you down, will you? "We'll do our best, but no promises."

The story of his life.

Never promise.

Chapter Nine

Mark and Don were arguing about how they'd keep the remodeling of her bathroom a secret. It's not like before when the supplies magically appeared while she was at work.

"You're going to have to tell her something. So why not try the truth?" Don asked while they hauled out the last bits of trash from the bathroom.

"The truth? Have you ever heard me tell anyone that?" Mark asked, but knew Don couldn't really answer. He always said something close to the truth, but unless he was being debriefed after a mission, he said his version of the truth only. Facts were not as important as telling the tale.

"Good thing we've been friends so long that I can see your bullshit story coming a mile away. But you better think of something, because we can't fix this without her noticing a major difference."

"I want you to call the hardware store again. I want you to tell your contact to say he has a tub shower unit and a toilet that got delivered to them by mistake, and the company won't take them back. They gave it to him at cost, and they want to know if Hannah is interested in taking it off their hands. Make up something like not enough room in the showroom or something. I know you, Don, you dish the bullshit just as good as me. I have faith you'll think of something."

"Brilliant. Yeah I know. I have to do all the labor, and come up with the plan. You're really not making this easy on me. This is a small town. People are bound to start talking."

"Let them talk. We'll be long gone before it makes it here."

"And if it slips out before then?"

"Stop worrying about what might happen and get the stuff. I have to be out of here before the end of next week."

Don looked at him puzzled, "Heading overseas?"

Mark shook his head. "Nope. Casey is getting married."

"Hell, no. Who approved this? No way our baby girl is getting married unless I give my okay."

Mark laughed. He'd had Don watch out for her anytime he wasn't able to. Came in very handy to know he could trust him to treat her like a baby sister and not some girl he was trying to hook up with. If he had, their friendship would've ended very quickly.

"I looked into him. Good guy. And he seems to be madly in love with her too."

"I didn't doubt for a minute that you *looked into him*.

I would've been shocked if you hadn't. I mean your poor sister could hardly date in school without you scaring the boys away."

"I know what boys are like at fifteen. Do you think I wanted any of them around my sister? Just because my parents said she could date at that age, didn't mean I wasn't going to keep a very close eye." *Casey may have thought I kept too close of an eye, but that's the job of a big brother.*

Don laughed. "You don't have to explain it to me, but I'm not sure Casey appreciated it so much. The only time she had any fun was when you were deployed and left me in charge. If it weren't for me, she probably wouldn't have gotten her first kiss."

"Don't remind me, Don. When I heard you let her and that kid go to the drive-in by themselves, I was going to beat your ass."

"Damn, you really do remember the details. I would've thought almost fifteen years later you'd forgotten that little incident."

That's the problem, Don. I don't forget anything. Even when I want to, I can't. He was no longer thinking of Casey. His mind was wondering back to Hannah and how gentle her voice was and how sweet her lips tasted . . .

"Mark, are you listening to me?"

The answer is no. "Sorry. Got a lot on my mind."

Don leaned up against the door jamb and asked, "Tenant or landlord?"

"Both."

"Hannah has had a real rough time these past few years."

Mark looked at Don puzzled. "What do you know?"

Don wasn't going to miss the opportunity to mess with Mark. "Oh, does Mr. Researcher need my help gathering information about his girl?"

Mark didn't find it amusing. He never mixed business with pleasure, well until now. Somehow they blended too closely, and it was becoming difficult to separate them. *Once I'm gone, this feeling will fade.*

"Is there something you think I should know?" His patience was dwindling and for good reason.

"While you were comforting Hannah, I had to hear about my lack of couth for delivering bad news from Bailey."

"I must be rubbing off on you."

"Exactly. I'm usually considered the nice one. Somehow Bailey thinks you're a nice guy, and I'm a jerk."

He didn't care what Bailey thought of him, but Mark found it humorous that she totally misread them both. *No one has ever mistaken me for nice.*

"There goes your big teddy bear image you've been working on all these years," Mark joked.

"It has to be this place, because, in a matter of days, I went from teddy bear to grizzly bear."

Although Mark enjoyed watching his friend suffer from this new revelation, he didn't see what this had to do with Hannah. "Was there a point you wanted to make about Hannah, or did you want me to listen to you whine a bit more?"

"Oh yeah, Hannah. I almost forgot. Bailey said I had no right breaking the news to Hannah like that because she'd been through hell and back the last three years. It's not only about losing her father either. From what Bailey said, she is carrying the weight of everything on her shoulders. That includes not just the house, which is bad enough, but all her father's medical expenses and funeral cost too."

That explains why she took in a tenant. She's desperate and now vulnerable. If that guy is what I think he is, he's more dangerous to her than I thought.

"How does Bailey know?"

Don said, "Best friends talk to each other."

He knew that was a dig at him for not sharing what was going on about the guy upstairs, but he didn't care. Some things he was unable to talk about, and other things, he just didn't want to.

"Didn't he have medical insurance?"

Don shook his head. "I asked the same thing. Guess he was self-employed as a carpenter, which makes sense with all the tools in that shed. But no health or life insurance. Hannah was at some university with Bailey in Rhode Island when she got the call from her father's doctor telling her how serious it was. From what Bailey said, they had extended family in Texas, but they only had each other in Savannah. So she left school, came home, and took care of him: financially, emotionally, and physically in this house until he died."

Amazing woman. She gave up chasing her dream for someone she loved. I always say I'd lay down my life for someone I love, but I guess that's the easy part. She has to live with what could've been but isn't. And yet she still has the smile of an angel and the strength of a lion. People underestimate my sweet Hannah. I wonder if she underestimates herself as well?

"That explains the issues with the bank."

"Exactly. Mark, that woman of yours spent every cent she had to give her father the best quality of life she could. Bailey said she wouldn't accept assistance from anyone then and never will. I'm only telling you this because when she finds out what you're doing, that woman is going to hate you."

I know. But better Hannah hates me, and I know she has everything she needs for a good and happy future, than she loves me, and I leave her broken-hearted. Because, I will leave. There's no doubt about that.

Her strength reminded him of his mother. Even though his father had ALS, she refused help in any way. Even from her children. He knew his mother didn't want to be in some Third World country during his father's last years, but she, like Hannah, was a selfless woman who cared more about others than her own needs. And, like Hannah, he worried about his mother, but no matter how much he tried, he couldn't save them. *Some things aren't in my power.*

"I know the risk."

"Bailey also said there is something else going on with Hannah, but she can't figure it out. Hannah told Bailey she's been suffering from recurring nightmares. When Bailey tried digging deeper, Hannah shut down."

It could be the loss of her father or the pending loss of the house, but I don't think that's it. What else is haunting you at night, my sweet Hannah? What is so troubling that you won't confide in your best friend? He was going to add that to his list of things to research, but for now, he wanted to address the major one at hand. *Her bathroom.*

"Don, get everything set at the hardware store for another delivery. Just remember, Don, this is her bathroom; I want the best, but not over-the-top because she won't use it."

"Got it. Double-wide, double-deep with Jacuzzi jets. And if you're lucky, Mark, you might even get a chance to try it with her," Don said as he was leaving the room.

Never going to happen. He couldn't help but turn toward where the tub would be going. *Although I can imagine how fucking amazing it'd be, to be in there with her.*

Mark slammed his hand against the wall and left the room. He didn't allow himself to fantasize. Reality and the here and now was all that mattered. And now he needed to head back to the other apartment.

While Don had been attempting to rescue Hannah's bathroom yesterday, he'd been with a member of his team, who'd dropped off some surveillance equipment. He was most interested in the listening devices. He knew he could have his team monitoring it twenty-four/seven, but that would raise a red flag. The guy freaked when he went inside the first time. Bringing in anyone new might spook him. It wasn't as though they were in a place where people just stopped by. They were as far off the beaten path as they could get. It was almost an hour drive to town. Brilliant if you wanted privacy, but not great if you're trying to blend into the crowd. *And let's face it. The men in my team don't blend into small-town USA.*

Mark knew he was going to need to update Don on what was going on. Unfortunately, it meant also giving him his spare weapon. If anything went down unexpectedly, he needed someone to watch over Hannah and Bailey while he dealt with the issue head-on. *I hope that won't be the case, but something is off. I don't know what he's doing upstairs, but I know he's planning something. I can feel it. No one has a row of cell phones on one table and a few laptops on the next. I need to find out who he is before I make my move.*

His cell phone rang. Pulling it out of his pocket, he shook his head before answering. "Casey, what's up?"

"Hello to you too," she teased.

If you're giving me a hard time, I know everything is okay. "I'm in the middle of something, can I call you back?"

He hated blowing her off, but wedding plans were the last thing on his mind. *I have all the information I need. She should call Mom if she wants to chat.*

"This will only take a minute. Since you didn't reply to my text message yesterday, I figured I better call you."

He saw it, but that was right before he walked in on Hannah's little meltdown. Getting back to her about when he was going to arrive for the wedding didn't make his list of important items.

"I know the time, Casey. You know I'll be there if I can."

"Why can't you come and stay a few days before the wedding? Kevin is going to be here, and so are Mom and Dad. I'd love us all to spend some time together."

It'd been a long time since they all hung out together. Maybe a holiday or two over the last twenty years. Their schedules usually collided. This time, he wasn't deployed, but he also didn't want to leave Hannah alone with the guy upstairs. *If I'd been here when he looked at the apartment, he wouldn't be a tenant. Just because you think you're safe, Hannah, doesn't mean you are. And nothing is going to happen to you on my watch. That I promise you.*

Mark was shocked at himself even for thinking the word promise, but something in his gut said it wasn't a slip, he meant it.

"I've got something I'm working on here, Casey. I can't leave."

"I thought you were doing construction for Sissie's cousin, Hannah. Is she that difficult that she won't let you go for a few days? I mean you don't need the job, Mark. If you can't stand her, then leave now and come here."

Oh, I can stand her all right. Too damn much. That's the problem. "She is not the issue. There are so many more repairs than we first thought." *Thanks to my little diversion tactic that worked like a charm, but with one casualty, her bathroom. Damn. I still can't believe I did that shit. Don's never going to let me live it down.*

"We? I thought you took these side jobs because you liked working alone. What's really going on, Mark?" She tried sounding in control, but he heard the concern in her voice.

I think she's spent too much time around me; she's picking up my interrogation skills. I don't like it. But what she still lacks is the ability to lie. You need both to excel.

"Don Farrell was between contracts and decided to come by and give me a hand."

"I haven't seen him in years. Not since you stopped making him follow me to make sure I was behaving myself." Casey laughed.

He was still around, just got better at not being seen. Don't worry, sis, I've always got your six.

"So get here a few days early, do you hear me?"

"I'll do my best, but I can't promise. We are in the middle of a major renovation, and I don't want to leave her here without a working bathroom. Casey, Hannah's had some tough times, and I'm not talking about needing work done here. I don't want to add to them." That was close enough to the truth to ease his conscience.

"What do you mean by tough times?"

"Her father died. She's trying to deal with everything, but I'm sure you can imagine, it's not easy." He knew that was going to hit Casey hard. She was taking their father's illness the hardest. She was Daddy's little girl. It sounded as though Hannah was the same with her father.

"I'm sure it's not easy for them."

"She's all alone, Casey. Her mother died when she was born." Even telling Casey this information was tugging at his heart. Empathy was something he often faced in the field, but this was unlike anything he's experienced. It felt *personal.*

There was a long pause on the line before she said anything. "Oh, my God. I've got it. It's perfect. I can't wait to tell Sissie. This solves everything." Casey's voice was beyond excited, and it scared the shit out of Mark.

What is she thinking? And what did I just get myself into? "Care to enlighten me?"

Casey laughed. "Not at the moment. I'll call you tomorrow. Have a great day, Mark."

She was too happy and plotting something. If he had the time to figure it out he would, but right now, he needed to help Don upstairs, or they'd never get this place done.

Mark flipped the button to record and left the room. Tonight he could listen while everyone else slept, except him and the tenant, that is.

HANNAH AND BAILEY were out for a walk when her cell phone rang. Not many people called, and usually it was a collection agency regarding her father's bills or her student loans. *What part of "I'll pay when I can" don't they get?*

She would pay every cent she owed. It might not be on the schedule they wanted, but she didn't like owing anyone anything. That's why she wouldn't accept charity. Because she was unable to return the favor. *One day things will be different. I will not give up. My father never did and neither will I.*

Her phone dinged announcing she'd missed a call. *They can leave a message that I can delete later.*

It rang again. *They're persistent today.*

"Aren't you going to answer that?" Bailey stopped walking and looked at her sternly.

What could she say, that she was avoiding taking the call? She pulled it out of her pocket and answered.

"Well, I thought for sure you might be preoccupied with that sexy contractor since you weren't answering my call."

Sissie.

"Sorry, Sissie. I didn't know it was you. How have you been?"

"I'll be much better when you get your pretty little butt over here to visit me. I've not seen you in a few years. I think you've forgotten all about me."

"Never. I've been so busy with the house and work."

"Excuses work on people who don't know you, girl.

Now my friend is getting married this weekend, and it's going to be a huge shindig. The whole town's invited with their families."

"That sounds exciting."

"It would be, but you're my only family. I'm not going alone. Do you hear me, girl? It's time for you to come and visit."

Sissie was using her tone that said *one way or another*. The problem was she couldn't afford to travel except to her job. Never mind traveling all the way to Honeywell, Texas to attend a wedding of someone she didn't even know.

"Sissie, I can't come right now. I'm sorry."

Bailey grabbed the phone from her hand. "Hey, Sissie, this is Bailey, your cousin's best friend. When do you need her there?"

Hannah couldn't believe this. Her best friend was turning on her like that. *She knows I can't afford to go. And I have all this construction going on. Bailey, you're not doing this to me.*

"Great. You'll see us both there tomorrow night. And thanks again for the invite. I've always wanted to see Texas. Hope the saying is true that everything is bigger in Texas." Bailey laughed, and Hannah was sure Sissie had a snappy rebuttal to that comment. Sissie normally was quick-witted.

Bailey ended the call and handed the phone back to Hannah.

"I can't believe you did that." Hannah's voice wasn't

harsh but shaking from hurt. She was going to have to call her cousin back and say she wasn't going. It would've been easier being upfront and honest the first time. *Now she'll be disappointed and won't believe I really can't go.*

"Do what? Get you out of this place and on a vacation you need so badly?"

"I can't afford to go, and you are the one person who knows that."

Bailey put an arm around her shoulder as they started walking toward the house. "You're right, but do you know what I do have?"

"No."

"I have enough frequent flier miles from all my flying to comedy shows that it won't cost either of us a dime to travel. And your cousin said we can stay with her. I know you took some time off from the diner so you could spend quality time with me. So let's spend it in Texas. Are you ready to give in, or would you like to come up with a few more excuses that I'll be happy to shoot down?"

"What about the repairs? Who is going to watch them?"

"Hannah. Be honest, girl. It's not the repairs you've been watching, is it?" Bailey laughed.

Damn it. This is why we're friends. She pushes me in ways I'm not always comfortable with, but she always has my best interest in mind. Am I that good a friend to her? I hope she knows how much I appreciate and love her. Once again she's right. I do need a break. "Okay. I'm going because I can't stand to share that bathroom with those two guys for another week. I only asked one thing, one small thing."

"Put the seat down?"

Hannah nodded.

"You have so much to learn, Hannah. It's the small things that trip up the guys. You'd have more luck asking for the moon."

Hannah laughed. "I'm glad you stole my phone from me."

"Good, because I have more to tell you, but I'm holding out till we're in Texas."

Oh great. And you're my friend? Hannah smiled and wrapped her arm around Bailey's waist as they approached the house. *Yes, you're my best and dearest friend.*

Chapter Ten

"**W**HAT DO YOU mean you're leaving me here to do the repairs on my own?"

Mark didn't look at Don. "I told you, Casey is getting married."

"Exactly. What I want to know is where the hell is my invitation? I thought I was like a brother to her."

"Don, men don't like to go to their own weddings, never mind someone else's. So tell me why you suddenly want to go?"

"For starters, there usually are a bunch of single women at weddings. Next, anything is better than sitting here by myself while you go off and have all the fun."

"You won't be alone. I'm leaving you here to keep an eye on Hannah and Bailey while I'm gone."

Don laughed. "So if I didn't have to watch the ladies I could go?"

"Yes. But I can't have them here alone with that guy upstairs." Don knew this could be serious as Mark had given him his spare sidearm. If Don weren't there, Mark wouldn't go to the wedding. His priority would be to protect them at all cost.

"Excellent, so we will take my jet, which is still at the airport."

Mark got up from where he was working and looked at Don. His voice was gruff and full of attitude. He was too tired to deal with any shit today. "What part of "you're protecting the girls" did you miss?"

"None. But since they're boarding a plane today, I don't see why I should sit around here twiddling my thumbs. Besides, it's a perfect time for me to have a crew come and get the work done for us."

Are they leaving? "Where are they going?"

Don shrugged his shoulders. "Bailey wouldn't say. She said it's a surprise for Hannah. I'm glad they're heading out of here. We can have this done in a week or less without killing ourselves doing it."

"What kind of surprise?"

Don was apparently frustrated. "I don't know, and I don't care. You brought me here to get the work done. Somehow it's all working out better than either of us could hope for, yet you don't seem to give a shit about what I'm telling you."

Mark knew Don was right. His focus was on Hannah and not on the house. *This trip is good. She'll be happy. That's all that matters. I just wish I knew where and why she was going. And why she didn't tell me . . .*

"What were you saying about the repairs?" Mark hated admitting he wasn't listening to Don, but it'd been obvious anyway.

"Since they are out for a week, I don't know why I can't bring in a team to get this all done. We don't even need to be here to supervise. They can show up in the morning, and we'll tell them what needs to be done and come back after the wedding, and we'll do the finishing touches long before the girls get back."

It sounded good. Mark liked projects, but this one was much more than he normally took on. Getting some extra hands while they were away would mean he could concentrate on the guy upstairs when they got back.

"Do it."

"Oh, I already did. They'll be here by six a.m. to-morrow. My jet leaves at ten."

Bastard. Don was the only person who could get away with pulling that type of shit and he knew it. But this time, he was more of a cocky bastard than usual. Even though the plan was coming together nicely, he preferred it when it was his plan, and he had control.

This has to stop. When we get back from Texas, I'm taking the control back. He knew this was much bigger than Don. He'd lost it with Hannah more than he ever thought possible. Time away from her was exactly what he needed. If he didn't put some distance between them, he wasn't sure he'd be able to hold back next time their paths crossed.

"Isn't this fun?" Bailey said as they stood by the window of the airport terminal.

"Loads." The sarcasm was coming through loud and

clear.

"Okay, tell me what's wrong."

Hannah turned to her and said, "I can't believe you wouldn't let me tell Mark we were leaving. What's he supposed to think?"

"Keep the man guessing. Besides, I told Don, and he'll tell Mark. See, all good. Stop worrying already."

Worry is all I seem to do lately. Worry about bills and worry about disappointing people. It's exhausting, and I can't keep doing it. But what options are there?

"It's easy for you to say. But that place is all I have."

"No. You're wrong on that point, my friend. You have so much more, and getting away to see your cousin might help you realize that."

I hope so. Right now I just want to be back at that old broken down piece of shit because that is where Mark is. That's stupid because he's been avoiding me since I had my little meltdown, but I can't stop thinking of him. The damn man is making me feel. I've tried so hard not to.

"While we wait for them to call out seat numbers, why don't you tell me what else you and Sissie have planned for me?"

"Good try, but no. That is a surprise. My lips are sealed."

"I thought we were friends."

"BFF always. But the answer is still no."

Before she could push any more, their seat numbers were called to board the plane. *You lucked out that time, Bailey. When will it be my turn to have some luck?*

They boarded, and Hannah gave Bailey the window seat. She hated to fly, but Bailey loved it. As they taxied away from the terminal, they passed by a row of private jets.

"Now that's the life. No lines, no waiting."

Hannah looked out to see what Bailey had been pointing to. "Maybe when we're old and gray we'll have one too," Hannah teased.

"It comes when you least expect it."

Then it should've already been here.

"Hannah, hurry up and look at that one. The smaller jet. What does it say?"

She leaned over again not watching the movement as they taxied, trying to avoid getting sick. "I don't know."

"Look. I think it says Farrell."

Hannah looked again. It did look like that, but she wasn't sure. The letters were too small. "It could be anything, Bailey."

"Yeah, it could, but it could also be Farrell. You don't think—?"

"No, Bailey. I don't. Did you see the old beat-up truck he's driving?"

"Oh, yeah. What the heck was I thinking? That some billionaire decided to play contractor at your house just for fun? I tell you, I think I've been doing comedy so long my imagination thinks anything is possible."

"Well, you ask Don when we get back if he's a billionaire undercover and let's see if he laughs." *I know I will if you actually do it.*

She gripped the armrest as they began their takeoff. Bailey reached out and covered her hand. "And off to live on the wild side for a week, Hannah. Who knows, maybe we'll even rustle us up some sexy cowboys."

She was going for one reason and one reason only: her friend with a very strong will. If she had her way, she'd have her feet planted on the ground where they belonged. She didn't know why she hated flying so much. She'd made this flight every summer when she was a child and went to stay with Sissie. But as she got older, things that hadn't scared her then, did now.

When did I change so much?

She knew the answer. It happened when she stopped dreaming of her future and living only in the moment. She hoped this trip would help her find the answers she was looking for. Find herself again. She might've missed out on her first dream, but that shouldn't mean there weren't new ones waiting to be made. All she needed to do was look past the moment and see what lay ahead.

That was easier said than done. She couldn't stop thinking about what she was leaving behind. Maybe when she saw Sissie she'd tell her about the promise she'd made to her father. Sissie was the same age as her father, so maybe she could shed some light on what she should do.

If she could let go, then she might be able to move on. It was the wise and healthy thing to do, but was she ready to or even capable of letting go? Only time would tell. Right now she was heading on vacation for seven days. If that didn't open her eyes to some major revelation toward her future, nothing would.

I already know what I want. I just wish I could have it. Time to grow up and think of things that are actually obtainable. Dad, you taught me to stand on my own two feet. Maybe I need to learn to lean a bit too. Might not be what I want, but maybe what I get instead.

"Hannah, you look stressed to the max. Close your eyes and sleep if flying is making you nervous."

Hannah didn't want to close her eyes. She knew what would happen if she did. The same thing that had been happening for the past three weeks, the recurring nightmare. The last thing she needed was to wake screaming on a plane and cause everyone to think there was something wrong then be escorted off by the police.

"You sleep, Bailey. I'm not tired."

"Hannah, you have bags under your eyes. And if you haven't realized it, I've shared an apartment with you before, and I know this is not you. I wish it was that sexy hunk of a man you have, but I don't think this has anything to do with Mark. Tell me what's going on. Why aren't you sleeping at night?"

God. I don't want to think about it. It is too painful and sometimes makes me physically ill. Why would I want to share that with anyone?

"We're friends, Hannah. If you can't tell me, go talk to a professional. But I suggest starting with me. My rates are cheaper." Bailey tried to lighten the mood to ease her tension. It wasn't working.

"Bailey, it's the dreams I can't shake."

"How long have you been experiencing them?"

"They started a few weeks before Mark arrived and each night they get worse." *Or at least they feel like they are. I can't tell any more.*

"Tell me about them. They say every dream has an alternate reason behind it. Let's see if I can decipher it."

"It's not a pleasant one." How was she going to tell her friend she'd been having nightmares about a man coming to her room and raping her? Just thinking about it made her hands tremble and her mouth dry.

Bailey squeezed her hand. "And you will feel better once you say it out loud. Let me try to help. What better time than on a flight?"

Hannah closed her eyes and visualized the dream as she spoke. "I get up because I hear something outside. I'm stumbling like I'm drunk."

"You don't drink so there is one thing wrong with your dream. Keep going and I'll find more."

There was nothing real about it, yet it felt so real to Hannah. It was like she knew something but her mind wouldn't allow her to see the entire picture. Forcing herself to continue, she said, "Bailey, I'm not alone, there are men in my apartment. People I've never seen before. One man is tall and strong like Mark and Don. He has dark hair and his eyes . . . his eyes are black and cold. Like staring into utter darkness. And his face. He has a long scar across one cheek, jagged and rough. I ask him what he's doing there. Someone shouts something to him, but I don't know what's being said. The man comes and grabs me, hurting me. His hands are digging into my arms as he drags me to my bedroom."

Hannah didn't want to think about it anymore. It was painful enough when it came to her in her sleep, but now recalling it hurt even more.

"Hannah. Have you ever seen this man before? In person or maybe on television?"

Shaking her head she answered, "I've thought long and hard, and no, I've never seen him or any of them before."

"How many men do you see in your dream?"

"Three, maybe four. But only one face comes back to me again and again. The one with the scar."

"What does he do in your dream?" Bailey's voice was so soft and sweet as she tried to console Hannah.

"He throws me on the bed. I try to move but my body can't. I try to scream for help, but I have no voice. His hand is on my throat and he says I'm his now. His mouth comes down on my lips, hurting me." Hannah felt sick as usual. "I can feel his hands on me, saying something I can't understand. I'm crying and want him to stop. Then the rest is blank. My dreams stops." *Thank God. I don't think I would want it to be any more than that. It's like dreaming of a rape that never happened. I know it's not real, but it is taking a toll on me physically and emotionally anyway.*

"Oh sweetheart. No wonder you can't sleep and look so tired. That's horrible. You must've watched a scary movie before sleeping one night and now you can't stop thinking about it. I've read about how some people are more susceptible to that after suffering a loss."

"So what do I do to stop the dreams?"

"One person said to write them down in a journal or diary. And this way they lose the power they have over you at night."

It sounded corny to Hannah, but she'd try anything. She was going to lose her mind if she couldn't stop the images each time she closed her eyes.

"It's worth the try. And Bailey, thanks for listening."

Bailey replied, "I'm glad I could be some help. Now sleep. I want you ready for those cowboys when we land."

Hannah laughed but it wasn't sincere. "Ready, willing, and able." *None of the above, but one white lie won't do any harm.*

She looked out the window. *Remember. It was only a dream. Focus on what's ahead and that's going to be a desperately needed mini vacation with Sissie and Bailey. Time to leave the bad dreams behind and fill them with some sweet memories.*

CHAPTER ELEVEN

*H*OW DID *I forget how hot it is in Texas? Dang, makes Savannah feel like a spring day.* As they entered the Wild Sass Saloon, Sissie practically leaped from behind the bar to give Hannah a big grizzly-bear hug.

"Sissie, you're going to crack my ribs."

"I need to toughen you up, don't I? Wait till these boys start draggin' you on the dance floor. You're gonna need to know how to stand your ground." Then she turned to Bailey. "I guess you're the young lady I need to thank for draggin' her here. Was she kickin' and screamin' all the way?"

Bailey laughed. "I'm hoping the bruises won't show because I brought my boots, and I'm not planning on fighting the boys off."

"Hell, yeah. My kind of gal. Did you spill the beans yet?" She nudged Bailey with her elbow.

"Nope."

Hannah looked at them both. "Are you sure you two haven't met before, because you're pretty chummy right now."

"Two peas in a pod." Sissie laughed.

"This is going to be a great vacation."

"For some of us," Hannah added.

"Don't you worry, Hannah. I promise you're gonna have a wonderful time. The three of us are goin' to a weddin' on Saturday, and you'll soon forget all your troubles," Sissie informed her.

I really hope so. "Whose wedding?"

"Derrick Nash, he's a local 'round here. A very sad story that's havin' a happy endin'. Not my place to tell it, though."

Since when? I know you're the gossip hound here. "Guess a lot has changed."

"Oh yeah. You noticed I had the bar spruced up? I needed to get with the times."

That's not what I meant. "Looks good. I hope you still serve your homemade lemonade."

"You bet I do. Just tell me, do you want it with a kick or without?"

"With," Bailey answered.

"Without," Hannah said.

"Go find yourself a table, and I'll bring them right over."

As Sissie left, Hannah turned to Bailey and said, "Am I going to forgive you for whatever little secret you and Sissie have?"

Bailey winked at her. "You've forgiven me for worse."

Great. That tells me nothing. Maybe I should've gotten

my lemonade with an extra kick.

As they sat listening to the music, a familiar face arrived.

"Don't tell me that's little Hannah Entwistle all grown up."

Hannah got up and greeted him with a hug. "Jack, you look great. I thought you would've moved away from here."

"Hell, no. I love Honeywell just like you love Savannah. You know it's home."

That it is. But love it, well that's not how I'd describe my feelings exactly. "Jack, let me introduce you to my best friend, Bailey Tasca. Bailey, this is Jack Bullard."

"Howdy. Any friend of Hannah is a friend of mine."

"Pleasure to meet you. Am I reading that badge correctly? You're the sheriff?"

Jack reached a hand up and tipped his cowboy hat to her. "Yes, ma'am. I'm the law 'round here, so if any of the boys get out of hand, you just let me know, you hear?"

"I like Honeywell already," Bailey said, grinning from ear to ear.

"So what brings you to Honeywell?"

"Visiting Sissie," Hannah answered.

"And we're attending the Nash wedding," Bailey added.

Jack said, "I didn't know you knew Derrick, Hannah."

"We don't, but Sissie said we were invited as her

family. So here we are."

Jack looked at her puzzled and turned to Sissie as she approached. She was grinning and gave him a playful wink.

"Yes, sir. These ladies have a special invite to the weddin'," Sissie said.

Special invite? Why special? I thought the family was invited. Am I missing something?

"Well, it's late, and my deputy needs the morning off tomorrow, so I best be heading out. I guess I'll see you two at the wedding."

"Looking forward to it, Sheriff. I'll save a dance just for you," Bailey said.

Hannah rolled her eyes. "If she only knew that you dance like an ox and will be stepping all over her feet."

Jack walked away shaking his head.

"Now there's the old Hannah I know," Bailey said. "Good to have you back."

Hard not to be when I'm around you. She raised her glass and said, "To a much-needed vacation."

Bailey raised hers and said, "To happy endings."

"Isn't that supposed to be happily ever afters?"

"Happy endings are fun. You should give them a try."

That's going a bit far, but okay. We are attending a wedding. "I think I'm going to follow Jack's lead and head to bed. I'm not sure if it's the heat or the flight, but I'm exhausted."

"Okay. You go. I'm still waiting for one of those

cowboys to ask me to dance."

"Bailey, they've been working all day and won't be asking anyone to dance till Friday night. Trust me. I know them."

Bailey looked disappointed and got out of her chair. "Heck, then I might as well get some beauty sleep. I hope your cousin's place has air-conditioning."

You and me both. But I don't want to get spoiled because going home won't be pleasant if I do.

"I CAN'T BELIEVE you had the men at the house so quickly." *Almost as quick as I can pull my team in for a mission. Now I see you have loyalty around your men as well. Different reasons, but still loyal men.*

"Why not, Mark? You think you're the only one who can bark orders and people jump? The only difference is, mine don't jump, they strap on a tool belt." Don laughed.

Not the only difference. But I get the point. "I'm impressed. You've got me believing that when we get back Monday morning, this place will be practically complete."

"Don't doubt it for a second. These guys are the best. If anything goes wrong, they'll have it fixed even before we hear about it."

Things going wrong are exactly what worries me. Hannah has to come back to this being completed. Her future is at stake, and I don't want to let her down.

"Quit worrying."

"I'm still trying to figure out what I'm going to say to Casey when she sees you at the wedding."

Don laughed. "Don't worry about it. I've already spoken to her. By the way, why didn't you tell me she was marrying Derrick Nash?"

"You know him?"

"Yeah. One tough businessman. I'm not sure how someone as sweet as Casey is going to handle someone like him."

"That was my thought at first, but Casey is not the little girl we knew. She's toughened up a lot. Been through a lot. Derrick loves my sister. When I was in Texas with them, I saw a man willing to die to protect her. That's all I needed to know."

"Guess we don't always know what lies beneath, do we? Because that's a man I never thought would get married again. Maybe there's hope for you yet."

Mark shot him a look. "Don't be looking at me. We're the same age and I don't see a wedding ring on your finger."

Neither of them were husband material, but it was for totally different reasons.

"That's because I enjoy the single life."

"And so do I," Mark said plainly.

"Then I guess we're both going to enjoy this wedding. Lots of single women."

"Yeah. Think about it, Don: a bunch of single women all wanting what Casey and Derrick have. And neither of us are going to give it them."

"Damn, Mark, why do you gotta ruin a man's dream?"

Because I live in reality, my friend. I don't lie to myself. That didn't mean he didn't deny himself things he wanted. Because he wanted Hannah, he just couldn't have her. Not the way he yearned to. "Don't worry. I'm sure you'll find someone who can put up with you someday."

"What's that supposed to mean?"

It means I'm done talking about it. "If you don't mind, I'm going to get some long-overdue, much needed sleep while we fly to Texas."

He closed his eyes, but sleep wasn't what he was after. He replayed everything he'd heard on the recordings of the tenant. The guy was smart enough to watch everything he said, but every once in a while he'd slip and say the transfer was made or payment was delivered and waiting on orders. Who they were paying and for what reason was crucial needed information. Since the guy didn't leave the apartment, he had to be doing it through someone else. This was some kind of professional ring. He wasn't ready to say a terrorist ring, but whatever it was, it was most likely illegal. He'd already sent some of the recordings off for analysis to see if they could identify any of the voices. So far nothing had come back. What he needed was a picture of the guy or a damn good description ASAP.

Just because Hannah was safe didn't mean his duty to his country was over. *I can't rest until I know what we're dealing with. Don wants to be back by Monday. I want to be there Sunday. Something isn't right, and I'm going to find out what.*

CHAPTER TWELVE

ALTHOUGH CASEY AND Derrick insisted, Mark and Don decided not to stay on the ranch. They both wanted privacy, but for entirely different reasons. Don seemed to think he was going to find some sweet young thing who wasn't going to be able to resist his charms. Mark wasn't about to remind him he wasn't all that charming. *Enjoy your fantasy buddy. I have no time for such distractions. Beside, there's one sweet thing already causing me enough distraction right now; I don't want to think about another.*

Now alone in his hotel room, Mark pulled out his phone and dialed his second-in-command, Johnson.

"Getting in isn't going to be as easy as you'd like to believe, Johnson."

"Never stopped us before, Collins. Other complications?"

"None."

"Right. So . . . the landlord and her friend?"

"Explain your hesitation."

"Just ensuring this is a duty mission, not one of . . .

love."

What the fuck? Mark wanted to jump through the phone and straighten Johnson's ass out. He had never questioned him like that before. All these years, he of all people should know better. *I don't love Hannah. I just don't want her hurt.* There was no way Mark was going to answer Lionel's *concern.* He was a damn good second-in-command but had crossed a boundary this time.

"Johnson, I have intel on a possible terrorist, POI. Do your job."

No matter how good the team was, they really had no idea what they were walking into. If anything went wrong, he wanted no civilians, especially Hannah, anywhere nearby.

"Hannah Entwistle and Bailey Tasca should be away until the end of next week, which provides time for us to get in and get out. If there is no evidence of criminal activity, no harm done, but if there is, we need to act fast. Just have the team close by so when I return they're ready for the mission."

"Roger that. The team is on standby if you need us. Text me, and we go in."

"Thanks." He slipped the phone back in his pocket and saw Don standing in the doorway. Johnson may have given him shit, but he was a good man, and there was no doubt he'd have Mark's back. He just needed to plan for the perfect time. *Get Don's men out of there and then we go in that night. One way or another, we are getting some answers before Hannah returns.*

"My jet is at your disposal anytime, Mark. If something is going down and you need to move quickly, you don't have to ask." Don handed him a business card. "The number on the back is the pilot's cell. I'll let him know to keep it fueled and ready for you."

He took the card and slipped it into his wallet. He normally traveled by chopper when a mission arose, but it wasn't a bad idea to have a backup plan. "Thanks."

"Still no name for the upstairs tenant?"

"Nope. I tried to get it from Hannah, but boy, that woman can be tight-lipped when she wants to be." *Or maybe she doesn't want to talk to me.*

"You need a new tactic," Don suggested.

"Mine has been working for years."

"This isn't an interrogation of someone suspected of a crime. If you haven't noticed, this is a sweet, innocent woman. I know this is going to be difficult for you, but you might want to try some humor or light conversation."

"What the hell, Don? You're making it sound like I'm some caveman who's never seen a woman before. I have plenty of experience."

"You're missing the mark. I'm not talking about sex. I'm talking about how to pet them to get the information you want. How do you think I knew about their travel?"

If you fucking tell me you were petting Hannah, I think I'm going to knock you on your ass.

Don must've read his mind as he raised his hands in

defense. "Bailey! I got the information from Bailey. Damn, man. You should know I'd never use my charm on your girl."

"Stop saying that."

Don looked puzzled. "Saying what?"

"You keep referring to her as my girl. She is not now, nor will she ever be, my girl. I am there for one purpose only, and that's to do the fucking repairs."

Don glared at him. "So you're all pissed about something that doesn't mean anything to you? Isn't that a contradiction?"

I know what the fuck it is. "You've known me almost all my life. In all that time have you ever seen me in a serious relationship?"

After a minute Don shook his head.

"That isn't by mistake. I choose not to become involved. My profession means I could leave a woman a widow. I don't want that." *Especially not Hannah. She's already suffered enough loss. She doesn't need to think about losing another person she loves. Hell, what am I thinking? I'm not the man she wants any more than I'm the right man for her.*

"I'm not buying that excuse. Tell me the truth: why are you still single?"

Because I've never met anyone I wanted that much. So what? I'm incapable of love. It works out perfectly for my job. No entanglements. I come and go as I please with no one to tell me no. I wouldn't have it any other way.

"Probably the same reason you're single, Don. No

woman would put up with either of us. Stubborn bastards to the core."

Don laughed. "Oh, I think you'd fall if the right woman came along."

"Okay, but you first. Remember, we never leave a man behind," Mark joked. Don joked about remaining single until the day he died, but Mark knew it was just a matter of time before he turned a new leaf and settled down. When they were young, Don talked about the type of woman he was going to marry. He even said he was going to have six children. *Turning forty in a few years, buddy. I don't know what you're waiting for.* Don would be a good husband and father. However, those were two things he never thought about for himself. He was in a routine that would be nearly impossible to change. *Damn. I'm thirty-eight. This old dog isn't about to change now.*

"Well, if that's the case, I think we should head over to the saloon and see if I can get a jump on it."

Mark knew Sissie. She wasn't a bad person, just too damn upbeat for him. There was no way he was going to be able to walk into that bar without her coming up and hugging him. He'd never been the hugging type, but Sissie wasn't the type of person to care. *I could warn Don, but that would take all the fun out of it.*

"To the Wild Sass it is."

As soon as they exited the hotel, heat slammed them in the face. "Damn it. How can people do this every day?"

"You're getting soft. Can't do a five-minute walk without your AC?"

"Just because I enjoy living the good life doesn't mean I'm incapable of roughing it. Or are you forgetting who you left upstairs in that apartment for hours while you handled other business?"

Even Mark found the cool air refreshing as they entered the bar. He quickly scanned the room but didn't see Sissie. *Maybe she's out. This might be our lucky day.* Mark had been there several times on his last visit. She had never left the place.

"Let's sit at the bar."

He was there but had no intention to get comfortable. He had too much on his mind. *Like what is Hannah doing right now? Why didn't she tell me she was going away? Did she think I wouldn't miss her? She'd be right, but weirdly, also wrong.*

Normally there was at least one person behind the bar. The bar was far from empty, so there should have been a waitress around somewhere.

"This is a bar where we can get a drink, right?"

Don apparently felt the same. The service was lacking. He wasn't an expert on how she ran her business, but this surprised him. "We can try the diner. No alcohol, but the food is good."

"Sounds good."

Both he and Don got up from their seats and were just about to head out the door when that high-pitched voiced echoed through the room. "Mark Collins, don't you dare try sneakin' outta here without givin' me a hug."

I was so close. Turning he said, "Wouldn't think of it, Sissie."

"Oo la la. Who do you have here with you?" She walked over and put her hand on Don's bicep.

Mark stood back and grinned. As she lifted her arms and pulled him in for a hug, Don gave Mark a *payback is a bitch* look.

"Y'all don't look like brothers."

"No, ma'am. Just a friend."

"From Buffalo too?"

"Yes, ma'am."

Sissie shook her head. "You two are so darn fine lookin' I'd think you're Texans who wandered too far north. What's your name?"

"Don Farrell. And you must be Sissie. My friend Mark wasn't able to stop talking about you the entire flight over. I think he missed you."

Mark shook his head at Don. *I'll fucking get you for that.*

Sissie ate it up like candy as she winked at Mark then linked her arms in each of theirs and said, "Well, you two are coming into the back with me. Me and my gals are shootin' some pool. They're pretty good, and I need y'all to come and distract them a bit, so I have a chance to win."

"Can I get a beer with the game?" Don asked Sissie.

"I tell you what. Y'all go down that hall and at the

end there's a private pool room. I'll bring you each a cold one on the house." She was off toward the bar.

"Welcome to the Wild Sass. I hope you know what you just did by agreeing to play whoever is in the back. It's probably some of her friends, who by the way, are just as . . . effusive as Sissie," Mark said as he headed to the pool room.

He opened the door and waved Don to enter then he followed. There was a woman with her back to them wearing a pair of short shorts, cowboy boots, her T-shirt tied around her waist. She was about to take her shot, so he stood quietly. She leaned over, so her upper body practically touched the table. Her fine ass was all he could see from where he stood.

Fuck. This woman reminds me of Hannah. Thinking of her, his cock started throbbing. He tried to concentrate on anything but the fine view he had. Mark heard Don speak very softly to someone behind him then the sound of the door closing. He was tempted to look over his shoulder, but Mark couldn't pull his eyes off *her.* He tried to focus on the pool stick she held, but he could only picture her slender fingers wrapped around his cock, stroking him. *And for some weird reason, probably because I had just been thinking about missing Hannah, I feel guilty. As if I'm cheating on her. Ridiculous.*

As she pulled the pool stick back, her shorts rode up even higher. *God, you're killing me.* If this woman didn't take the shot soon, he was going to come right up behind her and take one himself. There was no way she didn't know how enticing she was in that position.

When she took her shot, the ball flew off the table and onto the floor. He heard her moan in defeat as she laid her face on the table.

"Really? There must be a better use for this table than for me to knock balls around."

Hannah! Even though her voice was muffled as she spoke, he'd know it anywhere. *For that matter, I should've recognized that ass. Perfect.*

He watched her as she slowly stood upright, pulled her cowboy hat off, and shook her lovely blonde locks loose so they floated to her shoulders. When she turned around, she had a sweet smile he'd become accustomed to. Unfortunately it faded quickly when she saw him standing there. *Shocked or disappointed?*

Hannah looked around the room and asked, "Where's Bailey?"

"Don't know. Don't care." He had no idea how he would've missed seeing Bailey in the room. He was so fixated on her beautiful ass; the rest of the room didn't matter. He was in Honeywell, where crime was a parking ticket.

"What are you doing here, Mark? Are you following me?" she asked, planting a hand on her hip.

That sounds like something I'd do, but no. Not this time.

"I WAS INVITED."

"You mean Sissie invited you?"

He shook his head. "My sister is getting married Saturday to—"

"Derrick Nash."

Small world. "You know Derrick?"

Hannah shook her head. "No. Sissie called and said her friend Casey invited me. I'm invited because I'm Sissie's family. She said that's the way they do it here."

Oh, Casey. You're good. Too good. I didn't see this coming. I'll not underestimate you again. Mark knew it was a small wedding for immediate family only with an exception of a few close friends. This is why Casey stopped hounding him. She was making the arrangements on the other side. *I have a feeling this took more than just Casey and Sissie to orchestrate. Don, you and I are going to have a chat when I see you. But for now, I'm going to enjoy this sweet angel who keeps appearing in front of me.*

It was apparent she was as blindsided by this setup as he was. However, she still seemed puzzled. *Does she think this is a coincidence? Because, I don't believe in them. And knowing the people involved, I know it's not one.*

Softly he said, "You don't look as happy to see me as I am to see you." That wasn't totally true. Her words weren't warm, but he could see her nipples harden beneath her shirt.

Hannah laughed. "I can see how happy you are." She was blushing, and he caught her meaning.

You're playing with fire, sweetheart. Mark stepped closer to her. *Dare me to touch you. I'll fuck you right here on the pool table.*

He was only inches away from her, and she leaned back against the edge of the table looking up at him. "Don't you want me happy to see you?"

Hannah's eyes turned dark green, and her voice was barely a whisper. "Yes, I do."

Mark put his hands on her waist and lifted her, so she sat on the pool table as he stepped closer, positioning himself between her bare legs. "Is this happy enough?" His hard cock was pressed against her intimately. He needed her so badly he was in physical pain. A woman had never gotten him to this point.

Hannah looked around him as though she saw someone.

"What's the matter?"

She looked up at him. "Anyone could come in."

Begrudgingly, Mark turned, took three long steps to the door, flicked the lock, and was back between his girl's legs within six seconds.

"The door is locked. We're all alone, Hannah.

"Mark, we can't."

He reached up and touched her cheek with the back of his hand, then came down across her jaw. His thumb traced her bottom lip. "We can, but only if you want me."

Mark felt her tense and thought she was going to pull away. As always, she blew his mind. Her mouth opened, and her tongue came out and wrapped around his thumb. Her eyes fixed on his as she sucked his thumb into her mouth, closing her lips around it. He thought he was going to explode in his jeans. *Fuck I want her so bad.*

"Hannah." His voice was husky with need. He could only voice her name. The little control he had was quickly slipping away as she teased him with what he wanted.

He closed his eyes and pulled his thumb from her mouth, but before she could object, he replaced it with his lips hungrily taking hers. His tongue entered her mouth twisting around hers. When he pulled back, she bit his bottom lip gently, drawing him back to her.

Mark needed to feel her, taste her. He didn't care if the sheriff himself broke down that door; nothing was going to stop him now. She wanted him, yearned *for him*, and he was going to give her what she was begging for. There was nothing except their raw desire for each other.

As his kisses deepened and his tongue filled her mouth, she melted against him, her hands grabbing at his chest. His muscles tightened as her fingernails raked over his pecs. It felt so good to have her back in his arms. He shouldn't have waited this long. *Why resist what we both want? What we both need?*

Hannah wasn't holding back either. Her tongue darted against his and she moaned his name into his mouth.

He pulled away slightly. "Baby, you need to stop now. You're amazing, but my restraint is running thin. You better tell me now if you want me to stop. Otherwise, I'm going to take you right here, right now." He trailed kisses down her neck as he spoke. Mark offered her the out, but he didn't want her to take it.

Her only response was to pull his head closer to her neck and lower to her chest. *Damn, sweetheart. You've got me on fire.*

His hands reached out and lifted her T-shirt. They only broke contact long enough to lift it over her head. She was unbuttoning his shirt, but her fingers trembled and she wasn't going fast enough for him. He brushed her hands away, gripped the shirt and ripped it open. The sound of buttons flying in all directions could be heard. He'd never had such little patience before, but with Hannah, his need was great and his control limited.

Hannah's hands instantly roamed over his bare flesh. Every place she touched tingled. She wanted to take control, to please him, but Mark wasn't going to let her give without receiving first.

He removed his shirt and laid it on the table behind her. Then he pushed her gently back so she now lay on the shirt. Her hips were high and planted perfectly in front of him.

She reached for him, but he ignored her delicate hands. He removed her cowboy boots and tossed them aside then unbuttoned her shorts and slipped them down her hips then her legs. She was wearing a sheer red thong with little black hearts on it. *Oh. Fuck. She's so fucking sexy. Need to be inside her. Desperately . . . but she needs to be satisfied first.*

He could feel heat coming from her. He slipped the fabric to the side and traced a finger over her wet folds. *Slow and gentle*. But his body wanted it hot and fast.

Mark slipped a finger inside her, and she clenched around it. His cock was begging to be released and deep inside her, feeling her grip him as he rode her.

Her body was already on fire, and she arched her hips to him. "Please, Mark."

"Sweetheart, I want you to enjoy it."

She moaned again as he added a second finger inside her. "Mark."

His fingers entered her faster and deeper. Her moans were now cries of pleasure echoing through the room. Mark circled her clit with his thumb as his rhythm increased.

"Hannah," he moaned her name as pleasing her was pleasing him.

Her body obeyed and tensed, her legs shaking as her climax took control. Her head turned from side to side, her back arched high, and her fingers gripped his shirt.

Her breathing was ragged as she spoke. "Mark, I need you. I want you inside of me now. I can't—"

With one hand Mark removed her thong, then unbuttoned and unzipped his jeans and let them drop to his feet. This was not how he would've pictured being with her, but damn it was fucking hot. *She's fucking hot. A lady in the streets but a freak in the sheets. Love it.*

He bent down and pulled his wallet out of his back pocket. He flipped it open and thankfully found the foil packet. Sheathing himself, he stood between her legs.

She wasn't holding back. Her eyes were like her fingers earlier, raking over his body. Taking the head of his cock, he stroked her wet folds and slowly eased himself inside. He let her adjust to his size, not wanting to hurt her.

Hannah brought her legs up and wrapped them around his hips, taking him deeper. He let out a deep growl, and in one swift move he filled her.

She cried out, "Mark, oh, God. Yes, that feels good." She arched her back, bringing herself even closer to him. He gripped her hips and pulled her to him as entered her. He tried to go slow, but she urged him to increase the rhythm. His own need took over. He entered her hard and fast, holding her off the table to not hurt her.

With each thrust, she begged for more. He gave it to her. She was wet and hot, and his cock was throbbing for release. He held back, wanting her to come again, but with him this time.

"God, Hannah. You feel so damn good," Mark's husky voice whispered.

"Mark, you're driving me wild. I can't hold back any longer."

"Yes, baby, let go."

He could feel her body clench around him, pulsing, wave after endless wave. When one stopped, another began. She cried out his name over and over. Only then did he allow his own body to let go.

He had never released so powerfully. As his cock

pulsed, her body continued to stroke him tightly. He heard himself calling out her name until his body was sated. He collapsed onto her. They were both holding each other, not wanting to let go.

Mark finally lifted himself and kissed her gently asking, "I didn't hurt you, did I?"

She shook her head. "I can't believe we did this here. In my cousin's billiard room."

He looked at her, and she was blushing. Mark didn't want her to feel any regret. What they'd shared was amazing. Would it always be that incredible between them? How was that possible?

"I can tell you one thing."

"What's that?"

"You're a much better lover than pool player."

Hannah burst out laughing and wrapped her arms around his neck. "Should I show you what other sports I'm not good at?"

He kissed her again and said, "Maybe we can discuss it in my hotel room?"

He lifted her off the table and helped her get her clothes situated.

"I'm not sure I can go out there. What will people think?"

"That their pool game sucks compared to ours," Mark said as he took her hand in his and led the way out, his shirt wide open leaving the evidence of their wild time together still scattered all over the floor.

CHAPTER THIRTEEN

H ANNAH WOKE THE next morning with her legs
tangled with Mark's. *It wasn't a wild sexy dream
after all.* She almost wished it had been. That way she
wouldn't need to face her cousin and friend after Mark
and she christened the pool table. Honeywell was like her
hometown—small—which meant people talked. *At least,
I don't live here, so what do I care?*

The problem was she did. She'd never acted so boldly
or recklessly. Mark said the door was locked, but they
were in a public place. Sex in a public place was something you heard about, but never actually did. Yet, there
she was, teasing him and practically throwing herself at
him. If she drank, she could say it was the alcohol, but all
it had been was an uncontrollable raw need like she'd
never experienced before.

*That explains the first time, but what about the second
and third time here in his hotel room? At what point do I
stop making excuses and just admit it? I like this man, and I
did exactly what I wanted to do for once in my life.*

Hannah let out a soft sigh. It felt good to stop worrying about everything. If she were back home, she'd never be as comfortable and free with Mark as she was here. It was neutral ground. *It was one night. That's all.*

The room was quiet, and she wanted to slip from the bed and back to her room before he woke. They spoke last night, but the words weren't deep and meaningful. It was light and fun conversation. Neither having a past or a future to think about. All they had was that night. *An awesome night I'll never forget.*

She tried to pull her leg free from his gently.

"Good morning."

Darn it. "Good morning. I didn't want to wake you."

"You didn't. I've been awake for hours."

"Don't tell me that I snore, and you couldn't sleep," Hannah teased.

He slid an arm under her waist and pulled her even closer to him. "No, but you talk in your sleep. Would you like me to tell you what you said?"

Talk in my sleep? Since when? She was wracking her brain, trying to recall what she may have said. Had the nightmares that have haunted her come to life? It was the first night in weeks she hadn't seen that ugly man's face in her dreams. When she did sleep, the only face she saw was Mark's. *It was refreshing, amazing, and I want to dream like that every night.*

Should she tell him about the nightmares? He'd been so understanding and willing to listen to her in the past, maybe he'd do the same now? *But what if I'm wrong? No.*

Not unless he asks me. Something like that would scare a man away. Hey I dream about a man hurting me in my sleep. Don't worry, it's not you. Nope. Not telling him anything.

"I'm not sure I want to know."

"Scared?"

She shook her head. "No. Well, maybe a little. Okay, tell me because it's going to drive me crazy if you don't."

"You said that if I were ice cream, you would put whipped cream all over me and lick me from head to toe."

She raised herself up on an elbow to look at him. Was he teasing her? Did she really say such a thing? *Anything last night was possible. I was drunk on life.*

Reading his expression wasn't easy. If she did say it, there was no taking it back now. All she could do was go with the flow. "I'm not sure I believe you. If I did say it, then tell me this, what flavor ice cream would you be?"

Mark burst out laughing. "You win." He rolled over so he now lay on top of her. "But I'm going to guess you're a cherry vanilla type of girl."

She stared at him. How did he know so much about her? Did she really talk in her sleep last night? "How di—?"

"You forget that Don and I are eating out of your refrigerator at home. It's the only flavor in your freezer."

Okay, he's not snooping; he's just observant. Because if you guess what I keep in my panty drawer, beside panties, I am going to have to start using that lock you put on my bedroom door.

Her phone rang, and she tried to reach for it. It was impossible with Mark's weight on her. "It could be important."

Mark's phone was vibrating on the nightstand at the same time. He rolled back off her and sat on the side of the bed facing away from her. She was going to make some funny joke, but she'd felt his body tense when it went off.

He didn't look at her as he got off the bed and went into the bathroom with his phone in hand. "Sorry, I need to take this."

She lay there watching as he walked away naked. *What's that all about? Laughing one minute, and all serious the next.*

Hannah reached for her cell and checked her missed call. *The bank. You really know how to ruin a nice vacation.* She saw the voice mail but hit delete without even listening to it. Whatever they wanted, they could call back and leave her another message just like they'd been doing for the past week. She had a calendar and knew the clock was ticking for them to foreclose on her home. Constant reminders from them wouldn't change that.

If you really want to help me, find a buyer. It was easier said than done. Obviously, the house needed so many repairs, and no one would pay what she owed, so putting it on the market was out of the question as well.

The tension she'd thought she'd left in Savannah slowly returned. *Proof that a person can't run from their problems, as they always end up finding you. But that doesn't mean we don't try. And last night, I actually succeeded. Even if it was only for one night, it was wonderful. I wasn't Hannah Entwistle whom the bill collectors wanted. I was Hannah Entwistle whom Mark Collins wanted.*

She looked toward the bathroom door that was still closed. Whoever it was, Mark needed his privacy, and she could respect that.

Lying there quietly, her mind started thinking of all the people it could be. His sister or his friend, Don. *Why would he get so darn tense for either of them? It couldn't be them.* She closed her eyes, thinking. He didn't have a job, so she crossed that off the list too. Her eyes flew open, and she shot another look at the door. *A girlfriend or wife would sure as hell make him tense.*

Throwing the sheet off her, she got out of bed and quickly put on her clothes. She couldn't find her thong but at that moment, going commando was the least of her worries.

I can't believe it. He's not available. Oh, God. I am not innocent here either. I never asked. I just assumed, and that is a stupid thing to do. Was that why he kept his distance initially? And here I was practically throwing myself at him.

She pulled on her boots, slipped her phone in the back pocket of her shorts, and left his hotel room.

Now he can have all the privacy he needs. As far as I'm concerned, last night was just a one-time occurrence. It'll never happen again. How he decides to deal with it is his problem.

As she walked down the stairs and past the front desk of the hotel, an older woman smiled at her, but Hannah had nothing in her to give back. Forcing pleasantries was more than she could handle. It was bad enough she was going to be face to face with Bailey in about two minutes. Nothing slipped by *her,* so it was going to be truth time. *And it wasn't going to be pretty either. How could I have been so stupid? How much of what he's told me about himself, which now I think about it is next to nothing, was actually the truth? For all I know he's not even homeless. Maybe he lives with her but travels for work? Why would he be so cruel? Couldn't he see I already have enough that I'm going through? Was that all a con when he held me the other day when I was crying? Was that some game to earn my trust so I wouldn't ask questions? I'm such a fool. A damn fool.*

Embarrassment changed to anger as she wondered who else was in on this. Don was his best friend. There was no way he didn't know what was going on, yet he chose to remain silent. *Don't be playing that same game with Bailey. She's not one to mess with. Bailey won't walk out quietly. She'll raise hell, and you'd be sorry you ever crossed her. God, why can't I be more like her?*

She crossed the street and walked to the Wild Sass. Hannah used the side door to go upstairs to Sissie's apartment. She knew her cousin would be downstairs at the saloon at that time of day doing her inventory and bookkeeping. One thing about Sissie, she had a routine and stuck to it. *Small blessing.*

Sure enough, Bailey was sitting at the table, sipping a cup of hot coffee. By the bags under her eyes, she'd been out very late last night herself.

Maybe this isn't the best time for a woman-to-woman talk. She'll probably bite my head off for being so foolish. This conversation can wait till after our vacation. No need to ruin hers just because I'm miserable. But right now I need a shower to wash away . . . him.

"Nice to see you remembered how to get back here."

"Very funny, Bailey. But somehow I don't think you're all that surprised I didn't make it back last night. Any reason for that?"

Bailey laughed and held her head. "I may have had a small part in the planning. Someone had to give you two a push."

Yeah, right off a cliff. Thanks, everyone. "So who knows what?"

"Casey called Sissie, and then I stole your phone and grabbed Sissie's number. Don called Casey after I had a long talk with him about you and Mark."

"Is there anyone who doesn't know?"

"Jack knows. Derrick knows. I think that is it. But then again, your cousin knows so the entire town might know." Bailey laughed and once again held her head. "Stop making me laugh already. My head is killing me."

That explained the smile she received when she was leaving the hotel. This was so damn embarrassing. Everyone knew they were together, but did they know he's not available? *No, probably not, or they never would've partaken in it. These are good, sweet people. At least, they were when I was here as a kid. I can't picture any of them allowing Mark to play me like that. We don't do that in Savannah, and I don't think they do it in Honeywell either.*

"You said Casey, his sister, knows?"

"Yes."

That eliminated wife. Casey surely would've known if he was married. So we are talking about a girlfriend. He was so secretive with his conversation, she suspected either they were still together or trying to work things out. Either way, she wanted nothing to do with him.

"Bailey, can I ask a huge favor?"

Bailey rested her head on her folded arms on the table. "As long as you do it quietly, sure."

"Would you mind if we skipped the wedding tomorrow? I really am tired and would rather spend a night relaxing."

"Ask me tomorrow. Right now, I agree with you, but I think I'm Don's date. I can't remember. I have wet spaghetti for brains."

You might want to ask if he has a girlfriend too. I don't want you getting hurt. Not if I can help it. "Okay. I'll be in bed if anyone is looking for me."

"Don't worry. I'm not getting up to answer the door." Bailey got up and walked to her bedroom.

She'd never known Bailey to drink much. Was there something else going on that she hadn't noticed? *Damn. She reached out to me to come for a visit. I was so consumed* with my own issues I never even asked what was going on in her life. What kind of friend am I? She goes through all this to get me some time alone with a man she thinks would be a good match, and I don't even question her surprise arrival.

Hannah walked to her room. *Tomorrow I get my head out of my butt and get back to being the friend she deserves. But right now, I need a long hot shower, a good cry, and twenty-four hours of sleep.*

MARK HADN'T MEANT to leave Hannah alone for so long, but when he got the call he answered. It didn't matter where or when, it was his duty.

His first thought was Casey wasn't going to get her dream wedding with the family by her side. Thankfully he had several days to organize things before heading out. That meant he could still make it back to Hannah's house on Monday and ensure the repairs were complete and get that guy out before she ever returned. It would mean flying out right after the wedding. Casey would understand. *She has to. I don't normally get an advance warning like this. She'll just have to be happy I am there when she ties the knot.*

When he returned to the bedroom, Hannah was gone. He was tempted to call her, but he had too much to get done. It was best she went and rested. He'd see her tomorrow at Casey's wedding. *She knows where to find me if she needs me. And I hope she does need me again because I need her. But right now I need to make sure she'll be safe. I can't risk worrying about her fucking with my head on a mission.*

He called his team in Savannah. It was time someone went in. Even though he trusted them to get in and get out unnoticed, he wished he was there. All they needed was a picture and/or a name. Having neither left them trying to trace his cell phone calls, which hadn't been easy. The guy had too many, and they were burner phones, not easily traced unless you stayed on the phone long enough. *This guy might be good, but I know we're better. Get ready. We're coming.*

He updated the men on the situation. *Officially, no one knows what we're doing, but my team works as one. On duty and off.* All he could do was wait for the word. The next twenty-four hours would tell a lot.

Putting his cell phone back on the nightstand, he lay down on the cool sheet. He could still smell Hannah's sweet scent. If she hadn't left, he would've spent the entire weekend making love to her. *I have never shared my bed with anyone so responsive to my touch, my words. She's the right combination of sugar and spice.*

Knowing the effect she had on him, he was glad she'd left. A mission was fast approaching. Although this one was supposed to be in and out, there was no room for errors. And a distraction, sweet as she may be, wasn't something he could afford.

I can't bring her back to the hotel room. No matter how badly I want her, I can't. Best I leave her with the memory of what we shared, instead of giving her false hope there could be anything more than one night. One fucking amazing night that I'll never forget.

Mark flipped open his laptop. *Might as well work.* That he could depend on. Work. Routine. Control. Success.

But then it hit him hard.

Work was all he had.

All he was.

He'd *never* yearned for more before. It was an unfamiliar feeling, and he didn't like it one bit. It made him angry. *What the hell, man?*

He was angry at Hannah. *Why?*

He closed the laptop. *She fucked with my head. Something I've been immune to all these years. That can't happen. I serve the United States, not my hormones. Lust.*

No, it's time for me to bring my walls back online. I don't make the same mistake twice. And kissing her, making love to her was just that. A mistake.

CHAPTER FOURTEEN

S HE COULDN'T BELIEVE Bailey agreed to suddenly change her plans again. She apparently wasn't all that excited about a wedding either.

"I have watched enough friends get married. I don't need to watch people I don't know. But I would've thought you'd want to be there because of Mark. It is his sister."

"Yeah, but like you, I don't know Casey. I would prefer not going."

Bailey put the last few items into her suitcase. Then she sat on the bed and stared at Hannah. "I'm packed, but I'm not budging until you tell me what really happened last night."

Hannah was watching Bailey. "I love you dearly, but I don't want to talk about it." *At least, not now. Not here.*

"And keeping things bottled up inside you is going to help how? Trust me. I know from personal experience."

Hannah noticed Bailey's eyes were showing worry and pain. "You're right. So let's talk. You first. Why the sudden visit?"

"Aren't you happy to see me?" Bailey smiled, but Hannah knew it was a fake smile.

"Always. You're my best friend. But that means we lean on each other, not just one of us doing all the leaning. So tell me, Bailey, what's going on? Guy trouble?"

Bailey looked down and was very somber. Hannah's heart started to race. In all the years they'd known each other, she had never seen her friend with this expression.

This was no longer about Hannah standing her ground but about being a supportive friend. She joined Bailey on the bed, reached out, and grabbed her hand. "You're not alone, Bailey. I'm right here. Please, whatever this is you can tell me; we'll get through it together. You know how I jump to conclusions with the unknown. And it's always better than I pictured. Now spill."

It wasn't even close to the truth. Hannah usually downplayed things and found out later how wrong she was. Right now so many horrible things were going through her mind that there was no way it could be worse than she was picturing. *God, don't let it be.*

"I know, Hannah."

They sat quietly for a few minutes. Hannah wanted to give her all the time she needed.

"I was doing my monthly breast exam, and I found a lump."

"Did you go and get it checked out? I know people sometimes get lumps from too much caffeine, maybe it's from all that coffee you drink." She tried to control her voice as not to show her own fears. Bailey needed her to be strong now.

Bailey nodded. "I went for a mammogram and then they sent me for a sonogram."

"What did they say?" Hannah was holding her breath praying for good news. None came.

"It's abnormal. I need to go in for a biopsy."

Hannah's heart sank. She wanted to pull Bailey into her arms and tell her everything was going to be okay. That it wasn't cancer. It couldn't be cancer.

Don't cry. Be strong. She needs you. "Oh, Bailey, I'm so sorry. Would you like me to go with you?"

Bailey looked Hannah and said, "You have so much already going on. I can't ask you to come to Providence to hold my hand for a test."

"Of course you can. And you know, I'll be there too. That is what we do for each other. In good times and bad."

Bailey laughed. "For richer or poorer too?"

"Is there a richer option? Because I haven't seen that one yet," Hannah added, laughing.

"I stand corrected. For hard up, poor, or broke ass."

The both fell back on the bed holding their sides from laughing so hard.

Once they stopped, Hannah asked, "Tickets to Georgia or Rhode Island? Wherever you go, I'm going with you."

Bailey gave her a hug. "Let's get this test done and

over with. But after that, I want you to promise me one thing."

Hannah nodded. "Anything."

"I want you to try to work out whatever went wrong with Mark. I have a strong feeling about him, Hannah. But I know you. You run from what scares you, and loving that man scares the hell out of you."

And for good reason, Bailey. He's got my heart but I can't have his. Apparently it already belongs to someone else.

"One thing at a time, Bailey."

"Hannah, I want you to promise me. Right after the biopsy, you go to Mark."

"Fine. I promise." *But what I am going to say is not what he'll expect.*

"So now you go and break the news to your cousin that we're leaving, and I'll be right back."

"Where are you going?"

"I'm going to see Don. Don't worry; I'm not going to say anything about you and Mark."

"Are you telling him we're leaving?"

Bailey looked at her strangely before she sat back on the bed. "I almost forgot. We still need to talk about you and Mark. You told me to go first, now it's your turn."

No, we don't. "There's nothing more to tell. It was fun, but that's all"

Bailey said nothing. Hannah knew she wasn't buying the bull she was dishing. She had no choice but to sit back down. She would talk but not about everything. Not after what Bailey shared.

"There is no doubt in my mind, Hannah, that you genuinely like the man. I have never seen you like this with a man. You're normally indifferent to them, but with Mark, you blush at the simplest things and your eyes light up when you see him."

Hannah's feet were dancing. Bailey was right. She was different around Mark. He made her feel something she'd never thought she would. She was twenty-eight, but he made her feel like she had a schoolgirl crush. She daydreamed about him and peeked at him through the blinds of her window when he was outside cutting wood for whatever they were building upstairs.

Knowing the effect he had on her didn't change anything. It just meant it was going to hurt more.

"Bailey, it's not about how I feel. Mark isn't . . . doesn't want anything serious with me." That was the closest thing she could say without divulging her suspicions. The truth was, right now that's all she had. No facts, but it didn't look good.

"Did he say he doesn't want you?"

"No."

Bailey's voice was filled with frustration. "You're dancing around not saying what really went down. How am I supposed to understand if you don't give me the facts?"

"Because I don't want to think about it, Bailey. It's only going to make me start crying all over again."

"What did he do?"

"Nothing."

"Hannah, do I need to go and ask him myself, because God knows I will?"

Always the protector. If I had a big sister, I think she'd be just like you: loving, supportive, and bossy as hell.

"He has a girlfriend." *There. I said it.* She wasn't sure if she felt better with it out in the open or not. But by the look on Bailey's face, she was shocked.

"Did he tell you that?"

"No. When we were in bed Mark got a call, and when he looked at the number, he tensed up and needed to leave the room. He was gone for about five minutes when I decided something wasn't right."

"Maybe it was his sister or parents or—"

"Don?"

"No. I was with Don. But it could've been someone else. Don't jump to conclusions without asking."

She had already thought that through; what other explanation could there be? "It's not his family, and we know he doesn't work. But you're right. I need to talk to him. I'll do that after I get back from Rhode Island."

"Why not today? Why not now?"

"His sister is getting married in two hours. I'm sure he is busy with family obligations at the moment."

Bailey nodded. "Good call. But, I don't think Casey would encourage us to set you up if he had a girlfriend. Sissie is a good judge of people, Hannah. You know that. I didn't see anything to doubt in the Mark I met. If you're wrong, and I hope you are, you better not wait too long, or he might think you're not interested."

Since he hasn't reached out to me since I left his room yesterday morning, I don't think he's stressing over it. When Mark undressed me in the poolroom, I felt embarrassed about my body. But he called me beautiful and worshipped my curves. All night. And I believed him. I need to leave.

"Okay, can we go now? Please?"

"I want to run across to the hotel and say goodbye to Don."

"Are you two serious?"

"I have too much going on right now to think about something serious. It was fun working with him to get you and Mark together."

"If that is what I would have to look forward to with the both of you, maybe I'm glad you're not an item."

"Don't think we won't do it again if we need to. Give me ten minutes, and I'll be ready to go."

ONLY A SMALL intimate group attended the wedding, so Mark noticed immediately that Hannah wasn't there.

"Don, I know you know something. Spill it," Mark said quietly to the side as they watched Casey and Derrick cut their wedding cake.

"Are you asking about Hannah?"

"You know fucking well I am."

Mark's father turned and gave him a warning look. He knew this wasn't the place nor the time, but when they last spoke, Hannah was going to be there. If something happened, he needed to know.

Don kept his voice low. "They left right before the

wedding."

"Back to Savannah?"

"I've been told not to talk to you about it."

"Which you're going to fucking ignore and tell me," Mark growled under his breath. *Why is everyone willing to talk to Don, but not to me? I'm an approachable guy.* He almost laughed at himself. Approachable was not one of his traits. Arrogant. Demanding. Stubborn. Intimidating. All those and more. But never approachable.

"I'm sure you could get the information yourself if you'd call her."

Mark glared at him. "Talk."

"They are going to Rhode Island. Something Bailey needs to take care of. Then Hannah will be returning to Savannah alone. Is that enough information for you?"

"Do you know when?"

"No. Bailey was quiet about what's going on. I even tried using my charm, and she clammed right up."

Mark was glad Hannah was with her friend, but the timing could be tight for her return to Savannah. She was supposed to be gone a few more days than that. "Is all the construction going to be completed by then?"

"Cutting it close. I'll have my guys work some over-time this weekend. They leave Monday morning, just as we're coming in."

"Do you want to fly out Sunday to be sure they're on task?"

Don looked at him sternly. "My guys might only carry nail guns, but trust me, Mark; they know their shit.

Anything that can be done will be done."

Mark knew he came across as an arrogant ass. He could apologize, but it wasn't the first time Don encountered it, and it wouldn't be the last.

Casey and Derrick were walking in their direction. Although she had a smile on her face, Mark knew she was about to chew him out for something.

"Congratulations," Mark said, extending his hand to his new brother-in-law. As they shook hands, Casey stood there, arms crossed in front of her, tapping her foot. *I don't think you're waiting for a hug. Okay, let it rip.*

"Mark Collins, I can't believe what you did."

Me either. Whatever it is. I'm sure I did it. "Nothing should shock you. But what did I do this time?"

"You scared that lovely girl off."

"She had things to attend to with her friend. Not my doing."

Casey shook her head. "Foolish man. Of course, it was your doing. You hurt her, and she left. Do you really think she had something urgent come up that she needed to leave on a Saturday? Don't even answer that. Whatever they needed to do was only an excuse." She threw her hands up in the air. "Even Derrick knows it's ridiculous."

Mark looked at Derrick who appeared to be as shocked by Casey's comment as everyone else. He shrugged his shoulders.

"I'm staying out of this," Derrick said.

"I have to agree with Casey," Don added.

He looked at both men. "Really? Are you both going

to take her side?"

They nodded. "She's making sense, Mark," Don said. "So why don't you call her?"

"Why don't you all mind your business?" Mark's voice was much sharper than he wanted.

Kevin, Mark's younger brother, joined them. "What's got you all riled up?"

Great. Why don't we get Mom and Dad over here too, and we can all talk about what a fuck-up I am when it comes to women. He didn't want to discuss this with any of them because it didn't matter. What they had was amazing, but calling to fix it was only going to open a door he wanted to stay closed.

"Just a difference of opinions."

"I can help. Casey is right, and you're wrong," Kevin said.

"Do you even know what we're talking about?" Mark asked.

He shook his head. "Nope, but I'm smart enough to know better than to argue with a woman. Especially on her wedding day." Kevin raised his eyebrows at him with a *stop this shit* look on his face.

Damn. You're right. Mark hated that he needed his kid brother to remind him of that. *I can add insensitive jerk to my list of less-than admirable traits.* He saw the look in Casey's eyes. She wasn't going to stop until she heard what she wanted.

"Okay, I'll call her."

Casey immediately relaxed as though it was a done

deal. *Don't think this is going to work all the time. Your wedding is one day only.* He had no plan to call Hannah, but the present situation controlled his answer.

Once he agreed, the party was underway, and the rest of the night went smoothly. Hopefully, the rest of the week could work this well. *Finish the construction, get that guy out of that apartment, and Hannah will be safe. She'll be able to move forward with her life. And I will move forward with mine.*

If only that meant he'd be able to forget her. He smelled her scent in his bed last night, and it was sweet torture. Surely once the assignment was over, she'd simply be a memory. *A beautiful, sassy, intelligent memory with the hottest body I've ever seen.* She'd somehow burrowed her way into his thoughts, but he would refocus. He would.

Mark looked at his father. He looked tired. Was it from traveling back to the States? He knew what that trip did to him. He could only imagine what it did to his dad in his condition. Even though he tried to hide it, he saw his father's left leg give a bit, almost as though he was dragging his foot slightly.

Then at the toast to the happy couple, his father dropped his glass of champagne. He'd laughed it off that he'd probably had one too many, but he'd been watching closely all afternoon. His father hadn't had a sip.

Casey was beaming from her wedding vows and too happy to have noticed anything, but he and Kevin had exchanged glances throughout the day. They knew things were changing. Even though Mark wanted to book it out of Texas and head straight back to Savannah, he needed this time with his father. *A few hours won't change a thing. Right now, this is where I need to be. I only wish Hannah was here with me. Maybe it's better she's not. It would only have given my parents a false sense of hope. And they might as well get it through their heads, I'm never getting married.*

CHAPTER FIFTEEN

MARK HAD SO much running through his mind. He told his team not to enter the apartment because Don's workers were on site. That would open a risk they couldn't afford. But being back in Savannah totally changed things. He could do it himself without having to worry about Hannah getting caught in the crossfire.

As he and Don did their walk through the house, he was amazed at how much the construction crew had accomplished in such a short period of time. He'd seen shows on television where they totally remodeled a home in three days, and he thought it was complete bullshit. Now seeing this, he had to give Don credit. He and his crew were better than he thought possible. *No wonder he's in such high demand. He pulls off the impossible.* He felt proud for his friend.

They stopped at Hannah's apartment first, which had been freshly painted throughout. He made his way to the bathroom, which he hoped would be a place she could enjoy now instead of her small tub/shower unit that would've been good for washing a baby or a pet. No adult was ever going to soak in that tub. She now had a double-wide Jacuzzi tub. *Damn. Knowing what she looks like naked, I can picture her right now. And I'd love to join her.*

He needed to push those thoughts out of his head. He was going to be gone when she returned. Mark knew she'd be angry with him for lying to her, but eventually, she'd forget all about him. It wouldn't take long before some other man saw in her what he did. She was a beautiful, sensual woman who was smart and strong. No matter what life threw at her, she'd never quit. Hannah was going to make some lucky guy a wonderful wife someday. *She shouldn't be alone. She deserves to share her life with someone who appreciates all she has to offer.* This house was no longer a building waiting to be condemned. It was exactly what she'd asked for when they were first texting. He'd made it a home. A place she could share with someone. Raise a family and live happily ever after.

Happy. Just like she deserves. *Unlike me. Not my future.*

A happy life is what he wanted for her, so why the hell did it make him angry thinking about it? These last few weeks were all about making her dreams come true. Her happiness was all that should matter. *So why am I so fucking miserable? Am I that shallow that I can't see past my own desires? This is what's best for Hannah. Fuck what I want.*

He chose what he wanted long ago. The Navy was his life. There was no way a woman, no matter how perfect she was, could enter his life and turn it upside down in a matter of weeks. She might have time to get him out of her system, but he had only a few days. There was no way he could go on a mission in this mental state. At least, not if he wanted to be one hundred percent focused. Even Johnson had questioned him a few days ago. Mark's head hadn't cleared any from then. If anything, it was worse.

"What do you think?" Don asked from the spare bedroom where they'd removed the closet to make her bathroom larger.

"I'm impressed. She'll like it."

"You think she'll care that we removed a closet?"

"If you make your visiting company too comfortable they won't leave."

Don laughed. "That's not the sales pitch I'd use when telling her why we had it done."

Does everyone think I'm an idiot? "I know how to talk to people."

"Yes, you do, when you're looking for information critical to the safety of the good ole USA. But talking to a woman, no. You suck at it."

"I do fine."

"I'm not talking about getting them into bed, Mark. This one is special. You know it, but you're too damn stubborn or afraid to admit it."

Mark almost lost it. They might be best friends, but

no one had ever told him he was afraid of anything without getting knocked on their ass.

"This would be a good time for you to shut your mouth, Don. Consider Hannah off limits for conversation going forward."

"I'm not one of your team you can tell what to do."

"You're right. But the warning stands."

He valued his friendship too much to stand there any longer. Mark walked out of the room and went to check out the rest of the remodeling. The apartment upstairs was practically complete except for some moldings. There was about a day's worth of work to do. Once that was completed, there was only one thing left for him to handle.

As he left the apartment, he stopped at the tenant's door. *You're next. Be prepared. Tomorrow, I'm coming inside whether or not you let me.*

HANNAH WALKED THROUGH the small shops in Providence. Many talented local college students had their art displayed for sale, making Providence so beautiful and unique. You could find great paintings, clothing, and jewelry.

Bailey wanted to rest alone for a few hours after her biopsy. Although she didn't want to leave her side, Hannah understood. There are times you need to have privacy to process, no matter how strong and positive you try to be. For Bailey, this was one of those times.

She figured it was time to head back, though. Hannah wanted to be near her friend. She made her way up the old cobblestone street. She couldn't believe she used to walk this route several times a day and never felt a thing. Now her thighs felt like they were on fire. *I'm only twenty-eight. Why do I feel like a hundred?*

Hannah didn't understand her lethargy. The last few days she'd been exhausted. She no longer was suffering from the nightmare and the scarred man's face seemed to have vanished from her thoughts as quickly as it had come. She'd not thought of him since she and Mark had their wild night of passion together. Now she was awake, haunted by the memory of Mark's touch. *Sweet and tender and the most amazing sex one could imagine, but dreaming of something I can't have again doesn't help. It only makes for a restless night. A hot and restless night.*

It had been an emotional few days, but mostly for Bailey. For the most part Hannah had been able to put aside her woes and be there to support her friend. It was different from when she'd been her father's caregiver day in and day out. Yet, she felt like she could sleep forever. *Was my heart tired? Tired of the struggle and tired of the uncertainty? Put that away, Hannah. This is not a time to be thinking of yourself. Bailey needs you. You can go home and sulk later.*

When Hannah opened the door, her vibrant and positive friend was crying. She ran right over and wrapped her arms around her.

"I'm here Bailey. I'm here."

Bailey shook as she continued to cry. Hannah wanted to do something, say something, but the best thing she could do was hold her. When she was ready, Bailey would talk. Patience was something she learned from taking care of her father. If you pushed too hard, they shut down.

After about ten minutes, Bailey wiped the remaining tears and told Hannah what was going on.

"They said the needle biopsy wasn't successful, and I need to go in for a surgical biopsy."

Oh no. Not Bailey.

Her heart ached for Bailey. Each test would bring forth a new one. Telling her it was going to be okay wasn't fair to her. But she'd be there no matter what the results were. She honestly didn't know anything more than Bailey.

"I'm staying here."

Bailey pulled away and stood up quickly. "No, you're not."

Hannah was shocked. "Why?"

"Hannah. I am afraid of the results."

"I know that. And that's why I will be here with you for whatever they are. You can't ask me to leave you like this."

"We're best friends; I need you to go," Bailey said plainly.

"I don't understand. Why don't you want me here?"

Bailey came back to Hannah and held her hand. "You know I always spoke about finding my Mr. Right."

"Yes. You will, so—"

"Please, I don't want to think about that right now."

She understood. Thinking about a future that was filled with uncertainty was difficult, and it was insensitive for her to have said that.

"You're right. Sorry."

"Please don't say sorry to me. That will make me feel there's bad news coming my way."

Stop talking, Hannah. You're only making it worse. She's hurting.

"I need you to do something very important for me. Will you do it?"

She reached out and covered Bailey's hand with her own. "God, yes. Anything, Bailey. What do you want me to do?"

"Go back to Savannah. You might not be willing to admit it, but your Mr. Right is waiting for you there."

"I can't leave—"

"You have to. If not for you, then for me. I'm angry and sad right now because I don't know what the future holds. You have a chance at what I want. If you don't at least try to make it work, then you're wasting an opportunity I wish I had. So please, pack and go back. My biopsy is scheduled for a week from now. You can go and still be back here by then. But you need to do this."

Can't you ask me to donate blood or something?

Do hours and hours of research on biopsies and the possible results and treatment? I have missed having an active mind like I did at vet school. That's one dream I know I'll never fulfill.

I'm not ready to face him. What if he doesn't want me? It hurts already. I'm not sure I can handle any more hurt right now.

"Hannah. Please."

"I'll go. But I'll be back here, do you hear me?"

"Loud and clear."

"Good." Hannah reached into her pocket and pulled out the small white box that she had picked up on her shopping adventure earlier. She put it on the table in front of Bailey.

She picked it up. "What's this for?"

"I thought of you when I saw it."

Bailey smiled and opened the box slowly. Then she pulled out a delicate silver necklace. There was a small heart and a round flat medallion engraved with the saying, *"I am a better me because of you."* on it.

"Oh Hannah. That is so lovely. Thank you, and I feel the same about you."

Once again the tears started flowing, Hannah's and Bailey's this time. As they hugged, they shared how much they had learned from each other. Eventually, they conceded it was a draw. But Hannah knew deep down, without a shadow of a doubt, she was the winner the day she met Bailey. *If a person only has one friend in their life, and they are like Bailey, then they have everything they need.*

"Love you, girlfriend."

"Love you too, Hannah."

Leaving her was going to be hard. Hannah wasn't

close to where she could begin to process the reality of a positive diagnosis. So, for now, she would return to Savannah. *Will Bailey be all alone or will her friends, Whosie and Whatsit from work, be around? She hoped her friend wouldn't hide from people—not like what I have done. It had made for some very lonely days at home.*

Home. Facing Mark was going to be nearly impossible. She was still sorting out her feelings for him. If she sat back and closed her eyes, she felt more for him than simple friendship for the introspective man. Lust. *Was it just lust?* Yes, he was drop-dead gorgeous. The man was ripped. He was so serious most of the time, but when he smiled, his face transformed and there had been times where she'd been dazzled speechless. When he had held her in his arms those two times when everything had felt so overwhelming, she had felt so safe. Less . . . alone. It was easy to see how close he was to Don, even though they were so different in nature. Sissie had liked Mark too. Despite his deception, he was a good man. *I think. Was I attracted to him because I had been alone for so long? Do I even know the real Mark Collins? Is he hiding other things? Other things that will make loving him impossible.*

Oh no. No, no. no.

I love him. How was that possible over such a short period of time?

Loving a man who doesn't love you back was worse than never finding love in the first place. He hadn't tried to reach her since their night together. Something was more important to him than her. *I want him to wake thinking of me and go to bed doing the same. And all I feel now is he doesn't think of me at all.*

She wanted to go anywhere but back to Savannah. But she made a promise to Bailey, and she was going to keep it.

CHAPTER SIXTEEN

MARK LAY ON his back beside the couch, halfway under the coffee table, waiting for Don to return from the store. It had been months since his back had given out like this. One minute he'd been fine, then he sneezed and the pain dropped him to the floor. *How the hell can I bench over three hundred pounds and be taken out by a fucking sneeze?*

He was grateful this was happening now and not in a few days when he'd be on assignment. He'd been able to hide it from the Navy for the last ten years, but all it would take is one incident recorded in a medical file, and he would be done. They'd never let him out on another assignment. If he was going to be pulled from the field and stuck behind a desk, he might as well retire. He had his twenty years in already but was far from ready to quit.

The first time this happened he'd been with Don, hiking on Mount Kilimanjaro and they were halfway to the summit. It wasn't a place with immediate medical attention, and he learned quickly that resting was key to recovery. Rest and heat wraps were the only helpful things. Anything else would show in his drug test. Don understood his dilemma and hopped right in Mark's Jeep and headed to town to get what he needed. *I should've had him help me off the floor before I sent him to the store.*

Mark heard what sounded like the French doors trying to be opened. Had Don forgotten his key? He didn't hear his old Jeep coming up the driveway. *Hell, he wouldn't have had time to make it to town and back. What's he doing here so soon?*

He tried to get up, but the pain shot through him again. Mark couldn't recall his back ever being this bad. Usually he could still walk, although uncomfortably. This time it was locked up, the slightest movement felt like a knife in his muscles. It was totally debilitating. He had no choice but to lie there waiting for Don to come back. Mark thought about calling him a slow-ass when he finally saw him, but Don knew how damn unpleasant Mark was when he was in pain.

If he wasn't tense before, that changed quickly when he heard muffled voices that weren't speaking in English. It sounded as though they were near the French doors. *Why are they trying to get into my apartment instead of the one upstairs? Are they drunk or lost—these guys are no friends of mine.* A moment later he heard the glass breaking and the lock being turned. *Shit. That's not Don. And God, I hope Don doesn't walk in when they're here. I have no idea what's about to go down and Don being here is only going to be distracting. I know he can handle himself, but if these guys mean business, he's not prepared to do what needs to be done.*

Mark closed his eyes to concentrate on everything he heard. The creaking of the floor said they still were on the other side of the house. He tried pulling himself up again, but it was no use. If he couldn't go on the offensive, he needed to consider a defensive plan. He carefully pulled himself so the couch would shield him. He wasn't hiding, but lining himself for action. At this angle, no one would be approaching from behind. As long as they stayed where he could see them, he remained in control of the situation.

They spoke boldly as though they believed no one in the house understood what they were saying. *That's their first mistake. Never underestimate your enemy. But I've spent too many years overseas, and it's almost a second language to me. So keep talking. Let's hear your brilliant plan.*

"I'm sure they're gone," one man said from the kitchen.

"Better if they are not here, I think," said the other in the hall. "It'll save us the trouble of coming back to kill them later."

That turned his blood cold. One voice sounded all-too familiar as he'd been listening to it on the recordings and phone conversations for two weeks. *But who is the tenant talking to?* He knew there were at least two here in the downstairs apartment, but were there more?

I should've known there was more than one person.

Fuck. It explains why I thought he never slept. Mark was pissed at himself. He'd entered that apartment, trusting Hannah believed there was only one person. She was wrong, but he'd been foolish trusting unverified information.

This is what happens when you let yourself get distracted by a woman. You lose focus. This mistake could cost me my life, but I'll be damn if it's going to cost Don his. Or even, my sweet Hannah's. Not mine. She couldn't be mine. This is not her fault. All she did was show me that she wanted me. I was the fucking idiot who let her believe "we" were a possibility. And not only have I hurt her, but I may have jeopardized her life. I'll never make this mistake again.

He pulled his cell phone out and texted Johnson. "911. Made. Armed." He knew the team would come, but he wasn't sure if they would make it in time. *If they're not here to save my ass, they damn well better get here to save Don's.*

He heard them walking through the apartment, flipping over things. They were searching, and he knew it was only a matter of time before they found the surveillance equipment he'd set up in the empty bedroom. He hadn't locked it because he wasn't going anywhere. He never thought his back would give out at the same time the fucking assholes from upstairs decided to pay him a visit. He knew if they had any doubts before, it was going to be over soon. *What had made them check today?* He knew what his next move would be if the shoes were on the other foot. He needed to prepare for the worst.

Destroy the evidence then eliminate the witnesses.

"Do you see? I told you. This man is not here for construction. He is an American infidel. He's been watching us."

The sound of the equipment being smashed on the floor echoed throughout the apartment. The recordings were backed up on satellite, so he hadn't lost anything, but that meant what was going down next wouldn't be on tape. Grabbing his cell phone, he prepared to start recording. There was only so long it would record before stopping, so he needed to wait until he could record whatever evidence the Navy would need, in case Mark wasn't around to provide a report himself.

When the crashing stopped, he knew it wouldn't be long before they were near him.

Mark tried to figure out exactly how many people had entered. He was sure of two, but if there were more, he'd take out what he could before they got him.

Listening closely, he heard a sound that confirmed his fears. The click of someone checking ammo and removing the safety on their guns. They meant business, but so did he.

"Now we have to kill them," said the unfamiliar voice, getting closer to the living room.

Mark hit record on his phone. *This they will need to know.*

"We had to kill them anyway. They've seen and heard what we're doing," the tenant replied.

"And what about the woman, the landlady? Does she

know anything?"

"She brought these men here and said they were contractors. She set us up," said the tenant from the other side of the couch.

"But I have enjoyed her so much," said the second man, joining the other beside the couch.

"You risked everything with your foolishness. Your lack of control is disgusting. You thought nothing of the mission and only of your flesh. You're weak and have brought this problem to us all."

What the fuck are they talking about? Enjoyed her so much? Lack of control? Hannah hadn't said anything about someone hurting her. They are not making any sense. And who are we all? How many more are there?

"Then she dies too."

"Yes," the tenant replied. "Everyone who has seen my face must die. Understood?"

That is not going to happen, not while I'm still breathing. Mark shifted his body, reaching for his M1911, tucked in the back of his pants. Even the slightest movement of his back was excruciating, but he didn't care if the muscles ripped in two and he never walked again, he wasn't going to let them hurt Hannah.

Mark slowly moved his gun hand to rest beside the leg of the couch, so the gun wasn't visible. Once he knew who he was dealing with, those fuckheads were going to be sorry they threatened Hannah.

He knew he was supposed to take them in for questioning. There was one hell of an internal battle going on. *Does duty trump love?*

It was a punch in the gut.

Fuck, no.

He loved her.

Not the greatest time to come to this conclusion.

These men intended to kill him. That didn't scare him half as much as the feelings he felt for Hannah. But no matter what he felt, it didn't change who he was. *Non sibi sed patriae – Not for self, but country.* An old Naval motto Vice Admiral Hamden often said. It had stuck with his whole unit, and he used it with his team too. In a few days, he should be leaving on assignment. Each one with the same risk. He couldn't. He wouldn't ask her to live that way. *With fear, concern, and possible future heartbreak.*

The footsteps were very close now. *Focus. You only get one chance at this. Don't fuck it up.*

As one of them walked by the couch, he saw him.

"Fuck, the infidel has been here the whole time!"

Mark didn't move and kept his eyes closed. He didn't need to see as much as he needed to sense the motion in the room. His hand was on the gun, and he was ready, but the timing needed to be right. One mistake and the gun that was pointed at him would fire.

"Is he dead?"

The one closest to him kicked his leg.

Playing dead wouldn't work as he knew one would check his pulse and the gig would be up. That meant he'd be shot before removing the threat. *Not happening.*

He needed to protect Hannah. She wasn't due today, but Mark wasn't going to take the chance.

Mark pretended as though he'd been passed out and was just coming to. "Hello, I need help. Can you call an ambulance?" He waited long enough before asking, "Can you speak English? Help. I need help." He knew they understood, but they still hadn't caught on that it was a two-way street. *Stall a little longer until they are both in the line of fire. Come on. A few more feet to the left and you'll be all mine.*

"He cannot understand us," said the first. "We can leave him today. We can leave and plan how to dispose of them all."

"At best we are trespassers for entering an apartment other than our own, at worst we are caught carrying guns. We must move now. We cannot allow anyone to know what we were doing here. The money transactions will bring many questions if it is out in the open. We have worked too hard to buy the governmental officials. We cannot afford a setback. He dies now. And as the others return, they die too."

"What about all the men that were here over the weekend? They're gone. What if they talk?"

"They saw nothing. Look at this man. Look at his eyes. He is dangerous. The others were not. We kill him now."

As long as they were arguing about what to do, he knew no one would fire. Once they agreed, he would need to act quickly. He also wanted to find out what the hell they meant by paying off government officials. He needed to tread lightly with this information. At least he had it recorded on his phone, but which officials hadn't been divulged. And the bigger issue was why? Was it a cover-up or information? Whatever it was, they were willing to kill to keep it quiet. His gut had been right from the beginning. He should've acted more aggressively and brought his team in immediately. *Even if you kill me, you're not going to succeed with whatever you have planned. My men will be here any minute. But you're not going to be alive to meet them.*

Mark heard a car pulling up the driveway. He couldn't tell if it was the Jeep or not. *It could be Don. I'm not sure he would've taken the gun I gave him to town. Even if he did, I'm sure he's not prepared to defend his life so unexpectedly.* He got a sick feeling. One he hadn't thought of until now. *Oh God. If it's not Don, could it be Hannah? Surely not. She wasn't due back today.* His back muscles tightened again in pain. *I can't let them hurt her.*

"Or we use this to our advantage, make him believe we are on his side and kill him when he is no longer indebted to us for saving him. We'll kill him no matter what, but must it be today?"

A car door slammed shut.

"Did you hear that? We kill this one now, and take the other one unprepared."

He could tell they were getting flustered. If they shot him now, whoever just pulled up would surely take off. This was the opportunity Mark had been waiting for.

They were not in sync with what to do. That made easy pickings because their focus was scattered. *Unlike mine right now.*

While they were still arguing, one man turned away and his gun was now aimed in the direction of the front door. There was no doubt in Mark's mind that once the front door opened, the gunman would have a clear shot for an ambush. He could see the cold look in their eyes. They were ready to die, and ready to kill, but Mark wasn't going to let that happen.

Now or never.

Mark gritted his teeth, twisted his body, and grabbed his gun he'd stashed. Instinct and muscle memory kicked in as he shot twice without thinking about it. The first bullet went straight into the forehead of the man who had his gun drawn on him. Even before he started to fall, Mark got the second shot off with a direct hit into the back of the head of the man who had his gun trained on the door, waiting for someone to enter. There was no hesitation. He knew it was kill or be killed. One split second meant the difference between going home in a box or not. Mark didn't blink as they both dropped to the floor. This was who he was, what he did. Many people might not find it pretty, but what he did made it possible for people to sleep at night and to feel safe. If they really knew the dangers lurking, the entire country would be in a constant state of fear.

It wasn't time to relax, to drop his guard. Mark knew only of these two, but until this house was searched top to bottom, he wasn't going to rest.

The front door slammed, and bags dropped to the floor. Then silence. Mark waited. He was hoping it was Don, but then again, it could be more men belonging to this group. He wasn't taking any chances and kept his gun drawn, aimed at the hallway and ready to kill.

"Mark?" Don called into the house.

Thank God it's not Hannah. She didn't need to see this. Actually, no one does. It's not pretty, but it's reality. And ugly one that I see way too often. A flood of emotions ran through him as never before. Facing death didn't scare him, but he pictured Hannah's sweet face as those fuckers spoke. He tried to keep the feelings at bay, but they kept creeping in. He wasn't about to share that with Don or anyone else.

"I'm right where you left me."

Don came around the corner with Mark's gun drawn. His eyes widened as he came across the first man. Don kicked the guns away and stepped over the body, and then saw the second one closer to Mark. He did the same to his weapon. It was obvious both men were dead, but Mark wasn't going to questions Don's judgement. If he hadn't pulled the trigger himself, he probably would've done exactly the same. *Only trust what you did yourself. Others perceptions could be clouded, and that cost lives.*

"What the hell happened?"

"The tenants decided to do some research themselves. They found out the hard way. I don't like being threatened."

"I can see that. Is that all of them, or are there more bodies lying around throughout the house?"

"I only know of these two. But I can't go and search. I've called my team. Until they give the all clear, you're to stay exactly where you are. I don't want them accidentally shooting you."

"That's comforting. While we wait, want to tell me what the fuck happened? I was only gone an hour."

Don was surprisingly calm and displayed his usual biting humor. Mark was certain he wasn't quite as calm as he led him to believe.

"Something must have tipped them that they were being watched. Whatever it is that spooked them, it doesn't matter anymore. I wish I had an idea what they were doing here in the first place. This is not a place to blend in. Hopefully I'll know more when I get into their apartment and go through their computers and gear. They were armed, Don. Right here under Hannah's roof. All this time. Fuck."

"True, Mark, but you couldn't pick an easier landlord than Hannah."

That's so damn true. Someone needs to explain how risky that is. He watched Don pull out his cell phone and start snapping pictures. He expected Don to be upset, grossed out, or ill. This was not a behavior he'd ever seen before.

"What the hell are you doing?"

"Documentation is key to any investigation. Don't

you ever watch any of the NCIS shows?"

You can't be serious. Don continued to snap photos. He was right, but what the hell?

"This is no television show, Don."

"You're right. But I figure pictures first. Then I'll call the sheriff's office."

"No. No local authorities messing with this. This belongs to the Navy and Homeland Security. If you call them, I'll probably be spending time in prison, and I'd be lucky to get a phone call."

Don snapped a few more pictures then stopped. "I can't believe this."

"What?"

"My guys just finished this apartment. You've got blood splattered all over the walls, and the hardwood floor is going to need to be sanded and polished."

Now wouldn't be the best time to tell him about the French door glass, or what the spare bedroom might look like. Mark was shocked at how calm and cold Don was about all this and thinking of repairs needed. It was going to hit him later. He just didn't know it yet. *I'll be here when it does.*

The sound of the choppers overhead reminded him there would be some explanations needed.

"Don. Give me your hand. I've got to get the fuck off this floor before my team gets in here."

Don reached out his right hand to Mark and hauled him to his feet. *Fuck!* Mark's back felt like it was going to fucking snap, but it was good to be vertical again.

"If anyone asks, I got slammed against a door jamb by one of the guys in the scuffle."

"Yeah. I know the drill. If you want, I'll even hit you to make it look more believable."

It was good to know Don had his back, but even the thought of being hit by Don made him want to cry in agony. He'd broken protocol, and there were going to be some tough questions to answer. *At least, Hannah is not here to hear them.*

As SHE APPROACHED the driveway, the noise had gotten louder. She looked up and saw a military chopper heading in the same direction as she was going. *Strange. I've never seen that before. Where could they be going?*

As she rounded the last bend, she got her answer. The chopper was descending to her lawn, and men were leaping out with weapons drawn. Two more choppers were already on the ground. *What the hell is going on here? I don't get visitors, never mind a military invasion.*

Hannah slammed on her brakes. She didn't know what was going on, but she knew it was a place she didn't belong. *I knew I should've stayed with Bailey in Providence.*

Then Hannah remembered why she was here, to talk to Mark. *Oh, God. He's inside.* Without even thinking, she threw the car in drive and headed right for the house. Two men dressed in black blocked her way with their weapons aimed at her. She stopped her car and raised her hands. *I can't help you if I get myself shot.*

The men approached her car from different sides. The one who came to the driver's door barked, "Who are you? What are you doing here?"

"I'm . . . I . . . the . . . I own this place." She hadn't realized how much she was trembling until she tried speaking. "What do you want here?"

"Ma'am. This is official business. It is none of your concern."

His voice said he was in control and she shouldn't question anything, but Mark was in there, and she wasn't going to sit back and do nothing.

"Who are you after?"

"He's none of your concern."

Oh God. They are after Mark. But that can't be right. Homeless is not a criminal offense. And what is the worst he could have, an unpaid parking ticket? She needed to set them straight. "You have the wrong place. He wouldn't do anything wrong. He's a good man. Unemployed, but a hardworking man, and I'll vouch for him."

They didn't say anything. Only stared at her.

"Please, you have to believe me. He wouldn't hurt a fly. He's gentle and loving and sweet."

"Who are you talking about, ma'am?"

"Mark. Mark Collins, my . . ." She wasn't sure what to call him. Her lover? That sounded so damn cheap. Her boyfriend? No, that label was currently being used by someone else. Saying he was the man she loved but hadn't told yet definitely was more information than these men needed. "He's my friend."

She watched the two men exchange looks. One seemed amused and cracked a smile. Hannah found nothing humorous in this situation. Mark was someone she cared deeply about, and these two goons were standing in her way. This was her property. She had every right to go where she wanted. Heck, they hadn't even shown her any identification.

"I don't know who you think you are, but you're on my property, and I know my rights."

"You'll wait right here until the house has been cleared. Understood?" His tone reminded her of Mark giving her orders.

Hannah sat back in the seat and wouldn't look at either of them. There's only one thing she needed to know, and that was if Mark was okay. *Please be okay, Mark. I couldn't bear it if something happened to you. There's so much I have to say, and we didn't part on good terms in Texas. Is this a sign that we shouldn't discuss it? Were you doing something illegal that day when you took that phone call in the bathroom? Is that why my house looks like something from an action film just before it all went bad?*

As she sat in her car with her hands on the steering wheel, the men who had rushed into the house with guns now came out, but not alone. Mark was with them. He was walking with the help of the man in front, while a few others followed behind. The guns were pointed down, which appeared to be a good sign. But Mark looked anything but happy. Actually, he looked like hell.

He wasn't walking like himself, tall and strong. Something was very wrong.

Looking more closely, she saw spots on his white T-shirt and more on his jeans. As they moved closer it was evident what those spots were. *Blood! Oh no! He's hurt!*

"Get out of my way," she said as she opened the driver's door, slamming it into the man's shin. They might not let her drive her car to the house, but damn it, she was going to see Mark now.

Although she knew it must have hurt like hell, the man didn't budge. She shut the door again, and totally un-lady like, she pulled herself up in her seat, grabbed the skirt of her dress and hopped out the back. This was one of the times a convertible came in real handy.

She didn't look over her shoulder to see if they were chasing her as she ran toward Mark. Hannah wasn't ignorant that the men surrounding Mark held their guns firmly. If they were planning on shooting her, they better do it quickly because nothing was going to stop her from being with Mark. He was hurt, and he needed her.

When Mark saw her, he stopped, as did the others helping him.

"Hannah. What are you doing here?"

She pushed past the first man that had a hand on Mark's bicep while leading him out of the house.

"Let go of him. He's hurt. What did you do to him?" She put an arm around Mark's waist, and she felt him tense up and suck in his breath. "Did you beat him?" she asked harshly.

The man snorted. "No."

"Hannah, I'm okay. But why are you here? You're supposed to be in Rhode Island."

"I had to see you. There's something I need to tell you. Something you should know."

"What is that?" Mark asked.

She looked at the men. Declaring her love for him as he was being taken away by the military for God knows what reason probably wasn't the most romantic way to say it. But he'd be gone and this might be her only chance. Bailey was right. She felt for Mark in a way she'd never felt for another. That meant she'd fight for him and stand by him. It didn't matter that he had nothing. She didn't either, and he knew that. So what if she'd lose the house. As long as they had each other, the bank could have the building and anything else they wanted.

Hannah turned to the man and said, "Whatever he's done, I'm responsible; he works for me. So if you're taking him in, you're taking me too."

The man looked at her then at Mark. "Ma'am. You're not allowed where we're going."

Then he's not going either.

"Hannah, why are you here?" Mark asked, his voice firm.

She turned to Mark. His beautiful honey-brown eyes were dark and filled with stress. She wished she knew if this was the right thing to do, and hoped the guards didn't tackle her to the ground and beat her too, but she was going for it.

Hannah threw her arms around Mark's neck and felt him wince in pain. If they only had a few minutes, she was going to make them count. *No one's ever guaranteed tomorrow.*

"It doesn't matter to me what they think you may have done. I know you. You're so loving and gentle and kind and probably the most trust-worthy person I've met. I was wrong for running out on you in Texas. I didn't know what I wanted then. But I do now. That's why I'm here." She kissed him on the lips briefly then said, "I came here to tell you that I love you, Mark Collins. I love you just the way you are."

One of the men made a comment she didn't quite hear. But whatever it was, pissed Mark off as he darted him a look that said he better shut up.

Then Mark turned back to her. "Hannah, there's so much we need to talk about. But not now. There are things I need to take care of first."

"You don't have to face this alone. I'm here with you. Let me help. I'll vouch for your character or whatever you need."

As they spoke, more men came out of the house. Some of them were carrying boxes and she could also see another carrying sealed plastic bags with the word EVIDENCE written on them. *I hope they're not taking things from my apartment without a search warrant. But then again, what is in there to take? I have nothing of any value, and the worse they will find is a little something hidden in my nightstand drawer. And that's not illegal.* She didn't care, they could search all they wanted, there was nothing to find.

What she wasn't expecting was what the next set of men were carrying. They held two cots. Each cot had a long black zipped-up bag. She'd seen them in movies. They were used for removing bodies. It was evidence, but of a different kind.

Then she looked at Mark. "Are those—?"

He nodded. "Yes."

One brief word was all he said to her. Men carrying dead bodies out of her home and all he gave her was something she already knew.

"Did you ki—?"

"Yes."

She refused to believe that. Mark would never hurt anyone. All he wanted to do was protect her. Someone like that would never take another person's life. But when he spoke, his eyes were as she'd never seen them before. She couldn't explain it, but it caused a chill to run through her body. He was, even though injured, a man of power and control. It both excited and scared the hell out of her.

"Sir, we've got to go. The commander wants you debriefed immediately, and we want to clear out of here before the local authorities show up. If they do, they're going to ask questions that we've not been authorized to answer yet."

Sir? Why are you calling a prisoner sir? She looked at Mark and was confused.

"Don't tell me what I already know, Johnson. We leave in five. Get the bodies on the chopper and get them out of here. Tell the others to grab all the surveillance equipment. I know some of it was smashed, but I backed up everything we'll need for the reports. Leave nothing that says we were here. Understood?"

"Yes, sir."

"And everything out of that guy's apartment. This is our one chance to collect what we need to make it count."

Hannah's eyes widened with shock. Mark was speaking as though he was the one in charge. And the others were acting as though he was too. *None of this makes sense. You're a handyman. They're military. Why are they listening to anything you say?*

"What about your friend Don?"

"He can be trusted. He knows the drill," Mark stated firmly.

"And this woman? Should we take her in for questioning? After all, she owns the place."

She watched Mark's eyes turn dark, almost black. "Hannah had no prior knowledge of what her tenant was up to. Actually she still doesn't. And I prefer to keep it that way."

"I strongly suggest tha—"

"Then put it in your report that I declined your suggestion."

The man nodded to Mark before he started barking orders at the other men. She'd never witnessed anything like this before. *And I don't want to again.*

"Collins, the men found an unidentifiable white powder. It doesn't appear to be cocaine."

"Bag it and send it to be analyzed ASAP. These guys were doing something, but I know it's not drug running."

She was hoping Mark was going to explain what was happening when he turned back to face her. He didn't.

"Hannah, I need to go. Don is inside and will explain what he can. Right now, I need you to promise me not to say a word about what you just saw. Not to anyone, understand?"

She looked at him, not saying a word. Her ears were hearing, but she wasn't believing. *This isn't some spy movie. We're just regular, ordinary, boring people. So why all this suspense? Why the mystery?*

"I'll be back as soon as I can so we can finish this conversation." He kissed her on the forehead then turned to the man still standing next to him. "Johnson, three minutes and counting. Let's get these birds in the air before the sheriff gets here from town."

"Roger that." Then the man waved to the others, and they immediately headed to the choppers.

Mark was right behind them. She watched silently as Mark hobbled inside. No one was forcing him. He really was leaving. Worse than that. He was leaving without even responding to her proclamation of love.

That's because he doesn't love me. And that's good, because I obviously don't know the man like I thought I did.

The man I loved wouldn't have killed anyone. I don't know who you are, Mark Collins. But don't come back here; if you do, I won't be here.

When all the choppers were out of sight, Hannah turned and walked toward the house. She needed to be alone. There was too much to process and no information or facts to help. Don was standing on the porch, watching her.

As she climbed the stairs, he said, "I think you should sit out here with me for a bit and let me tell you about our friend, Mark Collins."

She wasn't sure she wanted to know. Hannah already knew he was a liar. What else did she need to know after that?

"Don, I don't want to hear any more lies. Not from Mark and not from you. So unless you're ready to tell me the truth, then I'm going inside and having one hell of a good cry."

Don reached out for her hand and led her to the porch swing. "You can listen and cry. But I'm going to tell you the truth. What you do afterward is your business."

She had no choice but to follow him as he half dragged her along. This was the first time she'd seen Don serious. Normally he was all smiles and jokes. *I agree, Don. Today is not a day for laughter. People were killed in my home. I need to know why, and I need to understand how Mark was involved.*

Hannah sat near Don, closed her eyes, and prepared

to hear the ugly truth. She wasn't going to judge him until she heard all the facts. But once she had them, she'd need time to figure out what she'd do with them. He obviously wasn't the man she'd thought he was. *And I really love that man. You broke my heart, Mark. And you don't seem to know it.*

"Just remember everything I tell you must be kept confidential."

There wasn't anyone she'd want to admit this to. How she'd let a man into her home and her heart, and she never knew who he truly was. She was a fool, and that was something she planned on keeping to herself.

"Let's get this over with."

"I'm sure by now you realize Mark is not just your average contractor."

No shit. "I do." Her voice was lacking any emotion. All she wanted was the facts. Things that she wished she'd heard from Mark, but since he couldn't be bothered to stay and explain himself, then she'd settle for second best.

"I'm not even sure where to start."

"How about with who the two dead people are."

"Mark suspected terrorists of some kind, but who and from where we don't know yet. Or at least, not that I've been informed. The Navy keeps many secrets from their best friends."

And lovers.

"What I can tell you was your tenant wasn't here for a room. Mark had been monitoring them all along.

Somehow they caught wind of it and decided it was time to take him out."

"You mean, they were going to kill *him*?" Her heart raced at the thought. She might be angry as hell right now, but she'd never want him hurt.

"Yes, ma'am. And from what I gather, not just him. While waiting for his team to arrive, he let me in on their conversation. I was on the target list as well as you. So before you question him on how he could pull that trigger, you better think of what would've happened if he hadn't. Those body bags would still be full, but you and I would be in them."

Hannah felt dizzy and thought she could vomit. She lived a quiet life; this was surreal. Don was as serious as they come, and that scared the hell out of her.

"Are we still in danger?"

Don shook his head. "Mark wouldn't have left if he felt there was any lingering danger."

I know that. I just had to confirm. "So Mark was here all this time to spy on my tenant?" It hurt. He'd gone to such great lengths, including Sissie, so he could be in this house. All the Navy needed to do was reach out and ask her permission. She loved her country and would've said yes. There was no reason for lies and deceit.

"You're wrong there. He was here because he needed some R&R. His job is mentally, emotionally, and physically demanding. Between deployments, he likes to help others, like you, who could use a handyman."

"Are you in the Navy with him? Is that why you're

here?"

"Hell, no. I couldn't deal with someone telling me what to do all the time. I guess that's why I'm my own boss."

"So he honestly was here to help me?"

"That he was. And that he did."

If you mean by destroying my bathroom and eliminating my one tenant, then yes he did. "I'm sure he tried his best."

"Hannah, Mark cares a lot about you. If he didn't, he wouldn't have dragged my ass down here to help."

"I thought you were hard-up, looking for work."

"No."

More lies. I can't deal with this. I don't think anything is the truth right now. "I don't understand any of this, Don. Why bring you here? He knows I don't have money to pay you. I don't have money to pay him. Never mind the type of cash it would take to fix up this dump."

"You might want to change your words when you see the place."

She looked at him puzzled. She'd seen it last week. Her bathroom was destroyed, and everything else looked like it was in as bad of shape. "I know you both did your best, and trust me, I appreciate it, but I'm a realist. I obviously only found that one tenant because they needed the place to hide out and not be noticed. No one in their right mind would want to stay here. Heck, I don't even want to be here."

Don got up. "Let's take a walk."

He went to the door and held it open for her. As soon as she entered, she saw the hallway had been freshly painted. No holes in the walls and the hardwood floors were shining like she'd never seen before. The banister looked brand new, though she knew it wasn't. *This is amazing.*

"Do you want to start upstairs or downstairs?"

Hannah was frozen to the spot. This was more than she expected, and that was just new paint. "Okay, let's start upstairs because that was the worst."

He led the way, and she slowly followed. The last time she was up there she'd gotten the puncture wound on her butt. It was her own fault for concentrating so darn hard on Mark's perfect body. *Were you using that body to distract me so I didn't know why you truly were here? If so, it worked like a charm. I have been used. That does wonders for my ego.*

She expected new paint but almost dropped to her knees when she went inside and saw the living room. It actually wasn't just livable but beautiful. It made her apartment look horrible by comparison. "Wow!"

"Go all the way inside. This is nothing. You need to see the rest."

Hannah wasn't prepared, but she listened and went to the kitchen. All new appliances where once there were only wires. Now there were cupboards and a ceramic tile floor. "I don't understand. How? I would've seen this being brought inside."

"You were at work."

That huge delivery truck. It was for me. "I didn't order this stuff, Don. And I can't afford it."

He ignored her and said, "The rest of the apartment is finished as well. Would you like to see downstairs now?"

No. Not unless you're trying to give me a heart attack. None of this is making any sense. "Don, I don't know much about construction, okay I know nothing, but I do know two people can't accomplish this in such a short amount of time."

"You're right."

"Then how?"

"I had my crew come in, and they did most of it in just a few days."

"Crew? What exactly do you do?"

"I have my own construction company."

But of course you do. She thought back to Bailey's comment about the private jet parked near the runway. It had said, Farrell. *No way. That couldn't be his.* She was almost tempted to ask, but then decided she didn't care. The one person she did care about wasn't here to tell her all that himself.

She followed Don downstairs to the apartment they'd been using while working. Going through it, she found it was much like the one upstairs. As she approached the living room, she stopped dead in her tracks. There were two huge blood stains on the floor, and the walls also were covered with the dark red spots.

That made her think back to Mark's clothes. The

blood was from them. He'd been that close to them. That close to being killed. She turned away and ran from the room. Don quickly followed. She was crying in the hallway when he approached her.

"Sorry. I wasn't thinking about that. I'm an idiot."

"No. I needed to see it." She sniffed and wiped away the tears. "I think I want to go and lie down for a bit."

"You might as well enjoy your new apartment too."

She looked up at him. "There was nothing wrong with my place, well except for the bathroom that you guys were going to fix."

"And fixed it is."

Hannah went and opened her door. Once again fresh paint filled her nostrils. They hadn't stopped at the bathroom as each room she looked in was freshly painted and the house was amazingly cool. *The air conditioner works.* Each room had been completely done over. She was going to save the bathroom for last as she'd already seen what the others looked like, she assumed hers looked the same as the other two.

When she opened the door, she found once again she was way off the mark. Her bathroom didn't look at all like it had. It had a walk-in shower with a stone wall, a double-sink vanity, and a Jacuzzi bath definitely built to occupy more than one.

"How?"

"We removed the closet in the other room. Mark hoped you'd like it."

I'd have to be crazy not to. It's beautiful. Like a luxury hotel, instead of my house. "It's all very nice, Don. Please tell him I said thank you. I'll pay him back someday." *Somehow.*

"You tell him yourself when you see him. But I'm glad you like it."

She turned away in awe of the room and looked at him. "Thank you too, Don. I know this wasn't all Mark."

"Hey. I needed a vacation. Why not here in good ole Savannah?" He laughed, but she could tell he was only trying to brush off his part.

If Bailey wasn't going through so much right now with her health, I'd tell her to take the advice she gave me and chase his butt down. But then again, he hasn't been forthcoming with the truth with her either. And right now, she doesn't need anyone in her life who isn't being straight with her.

That's exactly how she felt. She might love Mark, but he'd kept so much from her. The excuse that it was confidential information, only shared on a need-to-know basis, was only going to go so far. *I'm glad it wasn't another woman he was talking to that morning, but I can't compete with the Navy. I know some men are married to their careers, and the military is one of those jobs. I've seen him with his men. I'd have better luck competing against a super model than his team.*

It was who he was, and based on the fact that he got on a chopper and left her there with Don—that's who he wanted to be.

When Don left her apartment, she locked the door behind him. It wasn't something she'd ever done before, but the blood stains were still fresh in her memory and made her think differently.

So much has changed. I've changed. I'm not sure what to think or feel. It's like a sweet dream and a nightmare all at once. I don't think talking to Mark is going to fix anything, no different than him remodeling the entire house. It changes nothing. The bank will be happy to see it when they come to repo it next week.

Hannah walked into her new bathroom and started the tub. *I might as well enjoy it while I have it. Because just like Mark, this soon will be only a memory.*

CHAPTER SEVENTEEN

T HE HOUSE WAS so empty she couldn't stand it any longer. Don left a few days after Mark. He said he wanted to finish what he'd started. Which was amazing and she'd never be able to thank him enough for that. Her father's dream of having all four apartments finished and ready for renting was complete. The only issue was Hannah didn't want anyone there. Her poor judgement of character could've gotten them all killed. She should've asked a lot of questions, but instead, because she wanted to be left alone, she asked none. It was a mistake she'd never make again.

Mark still hadn't returned. *He said he'd be back, but the time frame on when was vague, and a week later still no word. Probably another lie. So why am I still holding onto this stupid hope that he wants me and wasn't able to tell me then because of his job?*

She spent days battling what to do permanently. Should she find an apartment in town and continue working as a waitress or go back to Providence and look for work there? *Or maybe it's time to try someplace totally different. A place for a new beginning because this is coming to an end.*

Hannah had never felt so alone as she did now. *Anything would be better than this.*

Putting down her book, she was about to head inside. She saw a black Lincoln town car pulling into her driveway. There was only one person in town who drove that. *Great. The bank manager has come to claim the property. At least, he'll be a happy man when he sees all the improvements. Too bad I won't see any of the benefits.*

She wished Mark and Don hadn't spent so much money and time fixing the place. It was making it so much harder now to leave. Before the improvements she wanted to be anywhere but this house. Now it was where she wished she could stay. *How ironic is that? You don't appreciate what you have until it is slipping through your fingers. Then it's too late. All you can do is mourn the loss.*

Hannah had been on an emotional roller coaster lately, and it was so much more than just the house. Losing her father started it all. Then saying goodbye to the one man she had ever loved was like another knife in her chest. And worrying about Bailey and what her test results were made her feel like her life was spinning out of control. *Again.*

Reminds me of the day my father called me to say he had some news. I had never felt such fear or pain. Even with all the uncertainty in my life, losing my Dad, and saying goodbye to Mark are scars I'm sure I'll carry forever.

She was tempted to toss the keys to the banker and

walk away, leaving everything behind. But this wasn't his fault. He'd been warning her for months. It was time to pay the debt. One she had absolutely no way of paying.

As he got out of the car and stepped onto the porch, she forced a smile and offered him a seat.

"Mr. Fitzgerald, I've been expecting a visit from you."

"I wouldn't be here if you'd returned any of my voice mails I've been leaving on your phone the last few weeks."

"I'm sorry. I guess I—" She wasn't going to lie. That's not who she was. *Just say it.* "I couldn't bring myself to listen to them. I knew what you were going to say, but that didn't make it any easier. I've come to love being here, and leaving is going to be harder than I thought it'd be."

"That's what's nice about having choices now."

Choices? That's a funny way to put it. My choice is to go willingly or have the cops escort me off the property. "Is it too much to ask for twenty-four hours?"

"To do what?"

Cry until I have no tears left. Oh, I've done that already over Mark. If Mr. Fitzgerald would've showed up twenty-four hours later, he would've found the house vacant anyway. Hannah had a place she needed to be tomorrow. But she wasn't planning on staying with Bailey. All she wanted to do was be a loving and supportive friend, then come home. *But home is no more. Maybe I can call Sissie. Or maybe I'll find a job in Providence.* Even though she knew this day was coming, she'd never thought about where to go. It was foolish but she felt if she planned it, it was admitting defeat. And until this very moment, Hannah held onto a sliver of hope. *And now I'm left with nowhere to go.*

"I just want to pack a few personal things I'd like to take with me to Providence."

"Do you need a ride to the airport? I'd be happy to provide you transportation," Mr. Fitzgerald stated.

You really can't wait to get me out of here, and you haven't even seen what the place looks like now. "I can manage myself, thank you."

She really couldn't believe how cold Mr. Fitzgerald was. For the past year, he'd been very understanding, even though his hands were tied and he couldn't turn the other cheek any longer. This day could've come so much sooner had it not been for his kindness. *I guess having to do this doesn't agree with you anymore than it does me.* She understood it was only business. The loan was way overdue, and foreclosure was the only thing left.

"You know how to reach me if you change your mind." He got up and was about to leave when he said, "I almost forget about the paperwork. That's why I came all this way."

Her heart sank. The final paperwork was turning the property that her father had worked so hard to keep, over to the bank. *Sorry, Dad. I genuinely tried. I didn't want to disappoint you. Honestly, you knew what I wanted before I did. I want this house. I want it to be my home. To raise a family here. You gave me everything I needed as a child, and I was too foolish to appreciate it. Until, now. Thank you, Dad, for showing me who I really am and where I belong. I love you and miss you so much.*

Mr. Fitzgerald pulled out the paperwork and handed it to Hannah.

She opened it but her eyes were too blurred with tears for her to be able to read it. "Where do I sign?"

"Sign what?"

"The foreclosure paper? Don't you need my signature?"

"This isn't foreclosure paperwork, Hannah. This is the deed to your home."

She looked at him puzzled. "I don't understand. The bank holds the deed until the mortgage is paid off. Why are you giving this to me now?"

Mr. Fitzgerald raised a brow. "Your loan is paid in full. That's why I've been calling you so you could come and pick up this document."

Paid in full. No way is that possible. She knew she hadn't won the lottery and hadn't made a payment in more than a year. *How could it be paid—?* "Mr. Fitzgerald, we both know I didn't do this. Not that I wouldn't have, but I financially couldn't."

He smiled at her and gave an understanding nod. "Yes, ma'am, I know."

"Please tell me." She could tell by the look on his face he wanted to. All he needed was a little push. Using her southern charm she looked at him with her green eyes pleadingly. "I won't be able to stay here any longer unless I know who was so kind to me and why."

It worked. "Mark Collins. Although, it was supposed to be an anonymous donation, but that kind of money had to be transferred. Therefore, I know his name." *Mark? My Mark?*

"*Why* would he do that?" Hannah asked softly, but it was meant for only her to hear.

"That, my dear, is something I cannot answer."

Those were things she was adding to her ever-growing *I don't understand* Mark Collins list. Everything he did was amazingly kind and sweet. But none of it made any sense. His actions when he left did not match everything else. *Which one is the real Mark Collins?* It was going to require deep thought and also a face-to-face conversation with that man. *If I ever see him again.*

"Never mind . . . thank you, Mr. Fitzgerald. Thank you for coming all the way out here to deliver this to me."

Before he left the porch, she was in the house looking for her cell phone. *Why is it when I'm looking for something in a rush, it's never where I think it is?*

Hannah searched the entire house. She wanted to call Mark and give him a piece of her mind. It was bad enough he remodeled her entire house without talking to her but to pay off her mortgage too? She should've asked when exactly the loan was paid off. Was it before or after Texas? Did he feel guilty for having sex with her and not calling afterward? Because if that was the case it only made her feel cheap. What she shared with him that night was special beyond words. She fell in love with him when she thought he had nothing, and they would have nothing together.

I almost wish he did have nothing. This would've been much simpler. He and I would probably be together now. Instead, he is God knows where and for all I know, never coming back.

Hannah threw herself on her bed, face first. *Even good news doesn't feel good anymore. I need to stop this pity party I'm in and get back to Providence. The biopsy is scheduled for tomorrow afternoon, and I'm not going to miss it.*

She heard her phone ring. It was close, but she couldn't see it. Listening carefully, she shook her head as she realized where it was. Reaching under the covers, she pulled it out and answered on the next ring. It was from a restricted number. Normally she avoided answering those calls as they were collections calls.

"Hello."

"Hannah. It's Mark." The line had so much static she could barely hear him.

Her heart skipped a beat, and she wished she could teleport through the phone to be with him. *Problem is I don't even know where that is.*

"I can hear you."

"I'll be back tomorrow."

She hadn't heard from him since he'd left about ten days ago. *Now he wants to come back and what, talk?*

Hannah wasn't going to be at the house tomorrow. She was leaving at dawn to catch a plane to Rhode Island. She'd promised Bailey she'd be there for her biopsy, and she wasn't going to change plans.

"I won't be here."

"Hannah. I need to talk to you. Just be there."

The line went dead before she could respond. Her heart was being pulled in two directions. But she knew she needed to go to Providence and be with Bailey. She already came back to Savannah to work things out with Mark. He didn't have time for her then, and now, she didn't have time for him. *Maybe that's a sign. Our timing is always off. It's not meant to be.*

She couldn't bring herself to put the phone down. Deep within her she'd hoped it would ring again. But it didn't. Hannah wasn't sure what to say if they did talk. Her feelings for him hadn't changed, but she'd learned things that had brought out a different level of emotions. She was still angry he took all control away from her. His heart may have been in the right place, but that didn't give him the right to do it. *It made me feel as though he thought I need taking care of. I'm not a child. Life may have thrown me some curveballs, but that doesn't mean I'm incapable of taking care of myself.*

The phone disconnecting was a good thing. At least for her. She decided to pack for her early morning flight. There was no way she could take her negative attitude with her. Bailey needed love and support right now, and that is exactly what she was going to get.

As she pulled out her suitcase from her closet, a box that was tucked away on the shelf fell to the floor. It was not one she'd seen before. It was an old cigar box, and she knew no one who smoked them.

She lifted the lid. It was filled to the top with paper. Bringing the box with her, she sat on the bed and started to go through it.

She opened the first envelope very carefully as the paper was very brittle. Her eyes widened at what she saw. It was a love letter from her mother to her father. *Why didn't I know about these?*

Hannah often wondered what her mother was like. Her father had told her stories, but it wasn't the same. As she read the letters, it was like her mother was coming alive for the first time. She was a strong woman who knew what she wanted and wasn't afraid to say it. She was bold and confident. *I'm neither.*

As she continued reading, she realized her mother embraced life like no other woman she'd met. *Well, maybe Sissie. She's full of life too. You have to be to own a saloon in Texas, and Mom had to live all the way out here with no one around but Dad.*

The letters showed her a different picture. They hadn't seen each other all the time. That was strange because as far as she knew both her parents were home together, but her mother continued to write, "As I count the nights, I count the ways I'll greet you," at the end of each letter.

But growing up, her father never traveled. He

worked in town, but that was as far as she knew he traveled. *Actually, I went away every summer. I've no idea what he did then. Did he travel for work?*

The more letters she read the closer she felt to her mother, and it was evident her father traveled for months at a time, working on an offshore oil rig. *Why didn't he tell me? Is that why he sent me away every summer? So he could earn enough money in three months to support us the rest of the year?*

It left her feeling loved more than before. Raising a daughter all on his own must've been difficult, but never letting her know what he faced and the sacrifices he made would've been very challenging. Until her father became ill, she had no clue how much it took to maintain this house. And if her father had taken all his time off and had gone to work on the oil rig, that explained why the house had deteriorated so badly. He probably started projects with hopes of one day finishing them.

I don't want to live my life filled with "one day I will" I want my life filled with yesterdays and todays.

She remembered another quote from her mother's letter. "One moment in your arms is like capturing a lifetime of happiness." *No wonder my dad never remarried. He and Mom had something so sweet, so special; I wish for that someday.*

Through the letters, she found something she would carry with her always: true love was something neither distance nor time could steal away, and it lasts long after a person is gone.

Carefully she packed each letter back inside the box. Her father never used this room, so she had no idea how they came to be there. Although she wasn't fond of cleaning, she knew she'd emptied out that closet several times over the years. *Actually, I had to when I downsized, getting ready to move out. There is no way I missed this. And how did I miss them all my life?*

She held it to her chest and squeezed her eyes shut. *Thanks, Mom. Somehow you knew I needed this now.*

Getting off the bed, she placed the old cigar box back on the closet shelf. She didn't close the door immediately as she wasn't sure if it was going to disappear as magically as it appeared. *Even if they do, I'll carry Mom's words with me always. Just as Dad did all those years.*

After reading them, she knew she needed to find time for Mark. Yes, there were things she wasn't happy about, but if she didn't give him a chance to explain then she wasn't close to being the person her mother had been. *Thanks, Mom. You set the bar. I hope I don't fall flat on my face reaching for it.*

Her plans weren't going to change, though. Tomorrow was Bailey's big day, and she was going to be there, no matter what. *This BFF isn't going to let you down. I promised I'd be there, and I will be. You're not alone, Bailey. No matter what, I'm here for you.*

As though her ears were ringing, Bailey called at that very moment.

"Hi, Bailey. I was just thinking of you."

"Thinking how are you going to be able to pull yourself away from the hunk, Mark, to come back to Providence?" Bailey teased.

If only you knew. But now is not the time to talk to you about it. "I'll manage." She needed to get the subject back to something that wouldn't require lying. "My plane is scheduled to land at nine a.m. I should be at your apartment by ten."

"Yeah. About that. They called and rescheduled me."

"No problem. You just tell me when and I'll be there." Hannah didn't care if they put it off one day or a month, as long as the results were positive.

"Actually, they asked me to be at the hospital at five tomorrow morning. The doctor decided to do a surgical biopsy so they can see right away what we're dealing with and if needed, they can—"

"I'll be there. I'll have to meet you at the hospital, Bailey, but I'll be there."

"Hannah. I already checked. There are no flights coming in tonight. I promise I'll call you as soon as I get out." She heard Bailey's voice trying to be strong, but there was a tremble in her voice that normally wasn't there.

"Bailey Tasca. I love you dearly, now shut up and trust me. I'll be there before you go into surgery. Understood?"

There was a pause, and she heard sniffles over the line. *God, I wish I could hug you right now. I never should've left you. No one should have to face this alone. And there's no way I'm going to let you.*

"Okay, Hannah. I'll see you in the morning. Love you, girlfriend."

Bailey hung up before Hannah could say she loved her too. Hannah looked at her watch. It was almost eleven in the morning. She googled the driving directions. It would take approximately fifteen hours unless she hit traffic. *I can do this. I have to do this. She needs me. And God, I need her.*

She'd been in the process of carefully packing for her trip, but now she grabbed things out of her drawer, not caring if they matched or not. She lifted her mattress and pulled out the emergency cash she'd hidden away. It wasn't much, but it would pay her gas and the road tolls.

Good thing I don't have time to stop as I don't have any money for a hotel. Hannah made a strong pot of coffee, threw it into a thermos, and packed her car. There was no time to waste if she was going to keep her promise.

As she sped down her driveway, she looked in her rearview mirror at her home. *Yes. That's home. I'll be back. And with any luck, I'll be back to stay.*

The drive was long and painful. At times her eyes burned from lack of sleep, and she thought she wouldn't make it. But once she hit traffic in New York she woke right up. Even in the middle of the night, the highway was busy. She was grateful she'd made it through before rush hour had hit or she never would make it to the hospital in time. As it was, she'd pulled into the parking garage only fifteen minutes before Bailey was supposed to go in.

She was running through the hallway asking everyone she met for directions. *I have to let her know I'm here. She can't go in thinking she's alone.*

"Ma'am. You can't go in there," a heavyset nurse called from behind the desk.

"I need to see my friend. I promised her I would be here. I have to let her know."

The woman asked, "What's your friend's name?"

"Bailey Tasca."

She nodded. "Are you Hannah?"

"Yes. Hannah Entwistle. Can I see her?"

The nurse shook her head. "Sorry, but they already took her down."

"I have to. I promised her."

"She told me you'd be here, and asked me to give you this envelope when you got here. She said for you to hold on to it until she was out of surgery."

The nurse handed her an envelope. Hannah opened it, and the necklace she'd given Bailey just before she left for Savannah was inside. A tear rolled down her cheek. Bailey knew that she'd be there, and this was her way of letting her know that.

"Thank you."

The nurse smiled. "Miss Tasca also put you down for her contact. The doctor will be out to talk to you once he has any information." She pointed to the coffee machine and the waiting room. "Go have a seat. You look exhausted."

That doesn't come close to how I feel. But sleep is not

something I can do. I need to see Bailey. Once I know she's okay, I'll sleep.

She took a seat and held the necklace tightly in her hand. Her eyes were closed, but only so she could concentrate on positive thoughts for her friend. *The doctor will come out soon and tell me you are okay. Then I'm stealing my friend and taking her back to Savannah with me where she and I can finally relax and reminisce.*

MARK PANICKED WHEN he pulled up in his Jeep and Hannah was nowhere to be found. She wasn't the type of woman to be out in the middle of the night. He did what anyone with his technical ability would do. He turned on the tracker for Hannah's iPhone. He'd meant to turn it off once the scumbag in the upstairs apartment was gone, but he hadn't seen her since that day. It was a good thing because it had come in handy.

What he hadn't expected was to find out she was in New York and heading northeast. He had tried calling her, but it went to voice mail.

He dialed Don.

"Not calling me for another vacation so soon, are you?"

Mark didn't have time for Don's jokes. He needed to figure out where Hannah was headed. "Do you have Bailey's number?"

"Yeah. Why?"

"Give it to me," Mark ordered.

Don stopped him right away. "Check yourself, Mark.

You're not talking to your men on your team."

He was right. Normally he took time off between returning stateside and talking with others. But this was a short get-in-get-out mission that only required him to be gone days, not months. Either way, it probably wasn't wise for him to be reaching out to Hannah so soon, but he couldn't help himself. He needed to see her. If the connection hadn't been so bad on the plane when he was flying over the Atlantic, he would've started the conversation then. But what needed to be said couldn't be said on a phone. *Or at least it shouldn't.* There'd been too much left unsaid that day. She'd told him she loved him, and he'd said nothing back. *I was such an asshole. I deserve her not speaking to me, but I have to try. I owe her a response. Damn. I owe her so much more than that.*

He was disgusted by his actions. Yes, he needed to get out of there quickly, but what would five minutes have meant? He left her there to see the blood and hear the details from Don. He could only imagine how that went over. Don was a good friend, but Hannah was a delicate flower. He should've taken care of his own business. Made sure she was okay before leaving. *Damn, I was relieved when Don emailed me, advising he'd had the walls in that living room repainted and new flooring put down. He'd done so much already, but I know he wasn't doing it for me, he did it for Hannah. And that's the reason I know he'll give me the information. For Hannah.*

But he thought he'd be back for a day before leaving. However, his commander had other plans since he'd broken protocol. Even though he took out the bad guys, that didn't mean what he did was right. And the Navy had no problem reminding him of that.

"Hannah's not here, Don. I need to know if she's on her way to see Bailey. It looks like she's driving through New York and headed northeast. Where does Bailey live?"

"Rhode Island. And don't tell me you're pulling the same shit you did on your sister on Hannah. Trust me. It won't go over well. Women don't like being spied on."

"Rhode Island. Damn."

"Where are you now?"

"Georgia. At Hannah's."

"Great. I'm in the air now. Just left the Florida Keys an hour ago. Want a lift?"

Fuck yeah. "I'll meet you at the airport."

"I'll let the pilot know. Besides, I wouldn't mind seeing that sweet young thing again myself. Oh, before you bite my head off, I'm talking about Bailey."

Don't worry, Don. I know you're not that stupid.

Mark threw his Jeep in reverse and broke every traffic law there was to get to the airport. He wanted to make sure he caught up with Hannah before she decided to go off the grid.

As soon as Don's jet touched down, he was on the runway and boarding before the pilot had a chance to file his new flight plan.

"What time will we arrive?"

Don checked with the pilot. "Be on the ground by

six. That is if she is stopping in Rhode Island."

His gut was telling him that's where she was going. *The gut never lies.* "She'll be there."

During the flight, Don updated Mark with how Hannah had taken the news on the renovations.

"So you're saying she was happy?"

"I'm saying she was shocked. You might want to keep a bit of distance between the two of you until you iron out a few things."

He didn't care if she kicked, scratched, or bit him. He had every intention of pulling her into his arms and telling her he loved her the moment he saw her.

"What did you find out about the two guys you knocked off the last time I saw you?"

There was so much he couldn't say. The recording had uncovered several government officials who had been receiving large money transfers, which had been filtered through these men. What they still hadn't learned was why. There had been one name on the list that made his blood boil. Jeremy Talroy, his sister's former boss. He didn't know what the connection was, but he knew that man was as slimy as they come. Nothing they could find out about Jeremy would shock him, but the investigation became a whole lot more intense and lengthy. A delicate internal operation, they needed to tread lightly until they figured out how deep the corruption went. Everything was on a need to know basis, and he and his team would be planted in key roles to gather intel. There were a few people he had to share the basic information with, as repercussions could still come their way. He'd made sure to give Derrick a heads-up with the findings as well as Ryan Watson, so he could beef up security around his daughter, Donna. That just left his sweet Hannah unprotected, and he was soon going to resolve that.

"It's big, but we don't have all the details yet. The investigation is being handled by Homeland Security." *That doesn't mean I am not kept up-to-date, but you don't need to know that.* "There is one piece I haven't been able to figure out what it's used for."

"What is that?"

"Ketamine. It was found hidden in the belongings of the second guy. It's a fast acting drug, primarily used by veterinarians as a general anesthetic. These guys were not vets so who the hell were they going to knock out with that?"

"Maybe put it in some water supply in the town?"

"That doesn't make any sense. Not enough to do any harm being so diluted. No they had a target, but who?" Mark wasn't going to give up until he had the answers. No one carried that type of drug around without a specific use in mind. He might not have the answer now, but he would figure it out.

"Mark, you like the impossible, so this challenge is right up your alley. You just let me know when you find the answer."

I'll tell you something, but the truth might not be it.

"Your re-enlistment papers must be coming soon. Have you decided what to do? You already have your twenty years. The offer to work for me is always there."

It was a decision he never had to think about before. The papers came, he signed on again. This time he'd held on to them. He wasn't exactly sure why. Maybe it was because all the issues that had gone down in Savannah. He'd been distracted before and never hesitated. Why now?

"I'll keep that in mind."

"We'll be landing in thirty minutes, Mr. Farrell," the pilot announced.

Mark pulled out his cell phone to check her location. "What the fuck?"

"Not in Rhode Island?"

"It says she's in the hospital."

"Hannah?"

Mark dialed the number and spoke to several people, trying to get information. No one could confirm she was there as either a guest or a patient. "If anything happened to her I'll—"

"Mark, you have no idea why she drove all this way. I'm sure it's not to go for a medical procedure. There has to be another reason."

The only other reason he could come up with was it had to do with Bailey. Don didn't seem to have thought of that scenario, and he wasn't about to bring it up. *I hope it's neither of them.*

Don had called ahead for a limo to meet the jet. "Are you sure you don't want me to stay? I can cancel my meeting in Boston and ride with you. Someone really should keep an eye on you right now."

For unknown reasons, I've come to realize I can't live without this woman, and she's not taking my calls and is now at the hospital. Yeah. I'm tense. And if something is seriously wrong, it's about to get a lot worse.

"I'll be okay once I see her."

Don looked at him strangely.

"What now?"

"Just wondering if you know it or not."

"Know what?" Mark asked, frustration filling his tone.

"That you love her."

Hi voice was sharp as he responded. "Don, just get this plane on the ground."

"I'll take that as a yes."

When the plane landed, Mark bolted it to the limo, barely saying goodbye. He was not going to rest until he knew she was okay.

When he knew she was driving, he didn't text her. But now, he was worried. He sent her a text message. **Are you okay?**

She responded which was a good sign, but with only one word. **Yes.**

He sent a second text. **Tell me what's going on.**

No response. *She's alive. She's okay. And I'll be seeing her shortly.* He didn't tell her that. The next time they had any words, it was going to be in person.

When he arrived at the hospital, he used the tracker to find her location. When he turned the corner, he saw her sitting in a chair bent over, her face in her hands, crying.

He ran right over to her and pulled her into his arms. "Sweetheart, what's the matter?"

She looked up at him, shocked but crying too hard to speak. She wrapped her arms around his neck and cried even harder. He held her so tight he was afraid he'd hurt her. Whatever news she just received it wasn't good. *Thank God, it's not her, but whoever it is, it's killing her inside. I can feel it. And I wish I could make it stop.*

"I'm here, Hannah. You're not alone anymore."

He held her until she released her grip on him. Then he got up and grabbed some tissues from the nurse and handed them to Hannah.

"Tell me, Hannah. What happened?"

"The doctor just came out and told me it's cancer."

He felt a stab to his gut. *You're so young. You can't have cancer.* He knew it was a disease that didn't discriminate on age, race, or religion. "I want you to get a second opinion. We'll go to—"

"It's not me. It's Bailey. She has breast cancer. The doctor told me she signed paperwork before the biopsy to have a mastectomy if it came back as cancer. When the surgeon went in for the biopsy, they found a mass. So they are removing one of her breasts now."

Tears started flowing again. He had no words to comfort her. Mark saw a lot of death in his life and knew words never eased the pain. All he could do was be here for her, and all she could do was be there for Bailey.

His phone beeped announcing a text message. He looked at it. "It's Don."

Hannah's eyes widened. "Don't say anything about Bailey. I shouldn't have even told you. If she wants anyone to know, it's her place to say. Please, Mark. Promise me."

Not a good place to be. Between a best friend and the woman I love. "He would want to know."

"Mark, please. I only told you because I—"

"You love me?"

She nodded. "Yes. I love you, Mark. We have a lot to talk about, and there are things you're not going to want to hear."

"I know. But you already said the one thing that matters to me. You love me." He reached a hand out to touch her cheek. It was still wet from her tears. "Hannah, look at me."

She lifted her head, and as their eyes met, he knew, without a doubt, she was the one.

"I love you too." Words he'd never spoken to a woman before. Always told himself he'd never say those three words. And now he couldn't picture not telling her every day of his life.

He wished they were someplace he could pull her into his arms and show her how much he loved her. Kiss her the way he yearned to. But this was a somber moment. Her heart was torn in two. He understood that and respected it. For now, he would sit with her and wait by her side. Later, he would show her.

Lifting her hand to his lips, he kissed it. "We'll get through this together, Hannah."

She leaned her head on his shoulder and said, "Do you promise?"

He had never told a woman he loved her, and now he was going to say something else he'd never said. But he wasn't saying it for any other reason except that he meant it. This moment was life changing for him. She didn't know it, but the people closest to him would. "Hannah. I promise."

CHAPTER EIGHTEEN

THEY HAD STAYED at the hospital until Hannah had a chance to see Bailey and know she was resting peacefully. Mark could tell Hannah was emotionally and physically exhausted. As he drove her Volkswagen to a hotel only minutes away from the hospital, she dozed off. *You're an amazing woman, Hannah. Driving yourself from Georgia to Rhode Island all alone to be by your friend in a time of need. Absolutely amazing.*

He went in, got them a suite, and went back to the car to find her still asleep. If it wouldn't cause suspicion he would've picked her up and carried her to their room.

Brushing the curl across her face to the side, Mark touched her cheek gently. "Sweetheart. We're at the hotel. Let's get you inside and to bed."

Her eyes fluttered and finally opened. "I was hoping today was just a bad dream. That Bailey wasn't—"

"I know. She's lucky to have you as a friend."

Hannah got out of the car. "No, Mark. I'm the lucky one. She's been there for me when my father got sick, and then again when he died. Even now she's sick but worried about me."

"How do you know?"

"Because she asked if you were with me. She didn't want me to be alone."

Mark smiled. *I like Bailey more and more as I get to know her.* "Then I'm sure she was happy to hear you're not."

Hannah nodded. "She said next time I go visit, I have to bring you with me. She has a few things she wants to discuss with you."

If she knows what went down that last day we saw each other, I'm sure she doesn't want to tell me what a sweet guy I am. Mark knew whatever she'd say, wasn't half as bad as what he deserved. He might be here now, but that didn't make up for the times he wasn't.

He pulled her suitcase from the back seat, and they headed up to their room. "Right now all I want you to think about is sleep."

"Mark, I can't."

"Yes, you can. You did on the way over here. Once your head hits that pillow, you'll be out like a light."

As he opened the door, she entered the suite, turned to him, and said, "You're right. I could sleep for days. But I don't want to."

"Why?"

"Because no matter how stressful you think my day has been, it won't get any better until you and I talk."

The last thing he wanted to do was make things any harder on her. "Hannah, it can wait."

She walked over and sat on the couch. "No, it can't. If anything today has shown me, it's that things like this shouldn't wait."

He walked over and sat beside her. There was so much to say, and he had no clue where to start. "Would you like to go first, or should I?"

"I will, because I have many questions and don't want you distracting me so I forget."

A woman on a mission. I respect that. "I'm all yours."

"Good."

He sat there waiting, but she said nothing. All she did was stare into his eyes. "Hannah. ask me whatever you want to. I'll answer anything I can."

"Mark, this isn't fair."

"What isn't?"

"I was so angry with you for hiding things from me, for pulling the control away from me with the house renovations, and the mortgage, and for leaving me without even . . . saying goodbye."

You mean without responding to you when you told me you loved me. I'm a complete asshole and don't deserve you at all. But I'm going to try to explain now and someday try to make it up to you.

"Hannah. First you have to understand who I am. My entire life has been focused on serving in the US Navy. Nothing has ever come before that. What I do is confidential, and I cannot share it with you. Not because I don't want to, but because I can't."

"I understand that."

That's the easy part. The rest won't be. I'm going to have to be honest with myself so I can be honest with her. He reached out and took her right hand in his. Her hand was so tiny and soft. She was stronger than most women, but still fragile. He needed to remember that as he spoke.

"I was between deployments when Sissie gave me the heads-up that you needed help with your home. There have been times in the past that I would seek out small jobs to help people for a few days to change my mindset when I returned to the States. If I didn't, I've been known to be a bit difficult to be around."

That was mildly put, but telling her I can be a controlling, demanding asshole isn't the way I want her to see me. Hell, I'm already trying to dig myself out of the hole I dug. Don't need to make it worse.

"So your place seemed perfect. Until I got there and realized it wasn't only a few days that you needed me."

"Yeah. I tried to explain it when we were texting before you came. I honestly never really thought you were going to show up so I left out some things."

Most things. "I normally would've told the person that this job was more than what I was looking for. When I saw you, I knew I couldn't leave you to face everything yourself. Of course, that didn't mean I could do it either. That's when I called Don. Everything I know about construction, he taught me." *If I didn't you still wouldn't have a running water.*

"Why weren't you honest and let me know what you were doing? Why not give me the option to say yes or no?"

"Because I knew you'd say no." He said it. That was the truth.

She looked at him puzzled then shook her head. "Are you saying that you purposely lied and manipulated the situation because you knew I didn't want your help?"

"Yes. I'm an asshole when you say it like that. All I wanted to do was lift the weight off your shoulders so you could start fresh. You'd been through a lot and all I wanted to do was help. There were issues with my plan, however with the time frame I had to work with, it was the most plausible. I wasn't thinking about how my actions were going impact your life in any way other than a positive way. Obviously I was wrong."

"Lying, Mark, never gets a positive result."

"If you would've asked, I wouldn't have lied. But I am very good at my job, which meant I was able to make things seem different from what they really were."

Mark was at time to damn good at his job. He could hear the hurt in her voice as she asked.

"Was there anything real at all? Or was everything including Texas an elaborate effort to keep me from finding out what you were doing to my house?"

"Texas wasn't supposed to happen. I didn't know you were there. When Don told me you and Bailey went on a vacation, I thought I could attend Casey's wedding and return to Savannah to finish the job and be gone before you got back home."

"So you're saying you didn't want to see me again."

This is going so badly. How is it I can interrogate some of the most lethal people in the world, but I'm cornered by one sweet lovely woman?

"Yes and no."

"Care to elaborate on that answer?" Hannah asked with frustration loud and clear in her voice.

"Yes. I wanted it done so I wouldn't see you again. But not because I didn't want to see you. The problem was I found myself thinking of you all the time. I have never let myself feel as I did then. Or as I do now."

She as searching his eyes for confirmation. He was who he'd always been. A person who couldn't be read. Yet he wanted her to see the truth within him. Mark wanted her to see the side of him that he never allowed anyone to see. After a moment of her staring at him, she must have found what she was looking for as she asked more softly, "What changed?"

The answer was so complicated and yet so damn simple. "You. I changed because of you. I have been focused only on my job, and now I see you too. You've got me dreaming of things I've never dreamt of before."

"Like what?"

He didn't answer.

"Tell me, Mark. Help me understand."

"My job means you never know what tomorrow brings. So I've never allowed myself to think beyond today. You changed that. Through your eyes I saw a home, a family. Things that would've scared the shit out of me before."

"And now?"

"It scares the shit out of me thinking that you might not forgive me for what I did. And my dream will stay that, just a dream."

Hannah quietly took in everything he was telling her. *Why would she take my word after I told her I manipulated her to get what I wanted? Maybe I shouldn't have been so damn honest about everything.*

"Being married to someone like me wouldn't be easy. You'd go periods of time having to trust that I love you and will do everything in my power to come home to you. That is why I didn't want to see you. You deserve someone who will be with you by your side every day."

"Wait. What? Married? Who are you to tell me what I deserve or want?" Hannah's spoke sharply.

You're right. I shouldn't.

"For starters, you're right. I would've said no about the repairs. I was being so stubborn that I would've lost everything just so no one knew how badly I really wanted it. What you gave me was a gift I will cherish always. But it is lacking something very important that you didn't think about."

"What is that?"

"It's just a house. Our love is what will make it a home."

Our love. Home.

"No sweeter words. So is that a yes?"

"Was there a question?" she asked with her brow raised and a twinkle in her eye. *God, I love this woman.*

How had I ever thought I could go a day without her in my life.

Mark slid off the couch and dropped to one knee. "I love you, Hannah Entwistle, but I want your name to be Hannah Collins, if you'll allow it. And you would make me the happiest man alive if you would do me the honor of becoming my wife. Will you marry me?"

Tears streaked down her cheeks as she shouted, "Yes! There's nothing more in this world I want than to be yours forever."

He pulled her onto his knee and kissed her. She wrapped her arms around his neck and held him close. When he pulled away she looked at him puzzled.

"Hannah, there's nothing more I want to do right now than to carry you to that bedroom and make love to you. But I think we both need something first."

"What is that?" Hannah said as she yawned.

"Sleep. You've had a long drive and a very stressful ordeal. When we do make love, I want us both awake enough to enjoy it." He kissed her on the tip of her nose as he lifted her into his arms and walked to the bedroom.

She yawned again. "I'm not really that tired." But her eyes were already fluttering as she let him undress her and slip her between the cool sheets. It took everything within him not to caress her, kiss her, love her the way she deserved to be loved. Right now he'd have to control his own desires. No longer would he think of anything other than her wellbeing. Quickly he removed his clothes and slipped under the covers beside her. She curled up facing him, and he fought his flesh from reacting. It was a battle he almost lost.

"We have the rest of our lives, Hannah. We'll be home in Savanah before you know it."

Hannah tensed and asked, "What about Bailey?"

Even now in her exhausted state, she couldn't think of herself, only of others. He wasn't going to be able to change that part of her, and he didn't want too. It just meant that he'd need to be the one to care for her.

From what the doctors had said, Bailey needed six to eight weeks to recover before the next phase. He didn't want to be away from Hannah any longer than his job already required him to be. There was only one feasible option.

"I can't picture a healthier environment for her than the clean, fresh air back home. I think she should come and stay with us." He knew he was being presumptuous, but he didn't want to live anywhere but with her when he was in the States. From her body language, he knew she felt the same.

Tears started coming down all over again. *I seem to make her cry a lot. I'll need to work on this.*

"Thank you for understanding me, Mark. She needs me, and I need her too."

Kissing her gently he said, "It's me who should be thanking you, Hannah. I've been living all these years, but only now am I alive."

She turned her face to kiss his bare chest. "Alive and awake I hope because I'm suddenly not all that tired."

His body sprung to attention as her fingers wrapped around him. When he tried to tip her head up to his, she pulled away with a sly grin and inched her way lower, kissing him all the way. *Oh damn.*

Mark knew all his resistance was shot as soon as her tongue touched the tip of his hard cock.

"Hannah."

"Mark, I've never. . . I want to. . . taste you."

Her tongue darted out and licked the tip of his cock again. Mark almost exploded knowing she'd never been like this with another man. He brushed her blond curl away from her face, and he watched her open her mouth and take him inside. He groaned as she twirled her tongue around his cock before hungrily taking him deep into her throat.

"Oh, God, Hannah, that feels so good." Another groan rumbled through him. His body tensed as her tongue pressed firmly against his cock, licking the length of him and back to the tip again and again.

This wasn't his first, but no one ever had his blood pounding with such raw need before. She knew how to please him and bring him to the brink of no control. Mark wanted to roll her over and plunge deep within her, but he was in sweet heaven and didn't want it to cease.

Her rhythm became more aggressive with each stroke. She took his large cock deeper than he thought she could and as she did her moans vibrated against him.

"If you don't stop now, I won't be able to hold

back."

"I know." Sucking faster, she brought him to the brink, and with her other hand, she was cupping his balls.

"Fuck," he growled and pulled her up off him. "You might be ready for this to end baby, but not me."

Rolling her over so she lay beneath him he said, "I could hold you every day and never grow tired of seeing your beautiful face."

"Promise?"

Mark looked down into her gorgeous green eyes. She'd stolen his heart and exposed what he never knew was there: a man capable of love. He would promise her anything and deliver always.

"Hannah. I promise to love and cherish you always."

"I can't think of a better time to start than now."

"Now and till the end of time," he whispered against her lips.

"I love you so much."

No words would ever touch him as those did. They gave him immense power, yet could drop him to his knees. "I love you too baby."

He needed to touch her, give her the pleasure she'd given to him. That and so much more. As his hands caressed her breast; her moans grew deep. He wanted her to tremble in his arms. He rolled one nipple between his fingers while he sucked the other, teasingly flicking it with his tongue. His body wanted to release, but not before she was satisfied fully.

Reaching one hand between her legs, he found her clit with his thumb and slowly circled it. *God, you're wet.* Mark loved the feel of her body trembling at his touch. She quivered as he slipped one finger inside her and pulled it back out.

Breathlessly, she begged, "Mark I need you inside me. I can't wait . . ."

He entered her again. He circled her clit, and she cried out in pleasure.

"Please . . . I—"

Her body jerked violently as he felt her powerful release gripping his finger inside of her. He continued to stroke her with his fingers slowly until her body began to settle.

His hard throbbing cock ached, and needed to feel her wrapped around him. He reached for his pants, which lay on the floor near the bed. He opened his wallet and realized he hadn't brought a condom. *Fuck.*

"What's the matter?"

"I don't have any protection with me."

"Do we need it? I mean do we want it?"

He looked down at her. She was serious. He'd never thought about a family. But he wanted a child with Hannah. *There wouldn't ever be a better mother on this planet than you.*

"No we don't," he answered.

She smiled up at him as she pulled him down to her.

Pressing his throbbing cock at her opening, he paused and looked her in the eyes. He saw his own desire matched in her. He could wait no longer.

Never taking their eyes off each other, he buried himself deep inside her. He captured her lips with his, blending their moans of pleasure together. He slowly began to move inside her. In all his years, this was his first time not sheathed. *Sweet heavens, this feels fucking amazing.*

As their bodies came together, again and again, he felt like he was making love to her soul as well as her body. He began moving faster and deeper; her moans grew louder with each thrust. He gripped her hips and met her again and again. Her body rocked with a second release, and he felt her clench around him, causing him to lose control. Plunging deeper into her, he shuddered with his release sending his seed spilling into her in a release more powerful than he'd ever experienced before.

As they lay holding each other, still panting, he held her tenderly. *If we don't make a baby today, then I know we will one day Hannah. Whenever it happens, the timing will perfect, just like you my love.*

CHAPTER NINETEEN

IT HAD BEEN three weeks since Bailey had her surgery, and she seemed to be healing well. Mark didn't understand the emotional impact this was all having on her, so he stepped back and let Hannah handle that. He tried to be there as a kind, supportive friend, but mostly he let the women do their thing while he monitored things with his team.

Progress was being made, but it was evident this was going to be a long-term assignment. He had waited for the right time to discuss the re-enlistment papers with Hannah. Things had settled down, and tonight was going to be the night. He needed to make the decision one way or the other. Since he'd asked her to marry him, this was something they needed to decide together.

His days of living on his own routine were over, changed forever. He thought that change was going to take away his freedom, and he'd feel a restraint he wasn't accustomed to. However Hannah was more of a loving, giving woman than he'd imagined. She respected his need for privacy yet was there to offer her support before he even knew he needed it. In a short time, she'd learned to read him better than his own team, who had served under him for many years.

Even though he'd asked her to marry him, he hadn't yet informed his family or Don. The only person who knew was Bailey and that was because she was staying with them. Hannah had so much going on, and if his family knew they would hover over her, trying to get to know her better. Right now he wanted her to himself. It may be selfish, but he was only willing to share her with Bailey, for obvious reasons. But he knew that would need to change soon.

Derrick and Casey had called and wanted him to come for a visit. His parents were now back in Buffalo and wanted the same. Kevin was the only one in the loop with what he'd found and what he was working on, so they spoke frequently, but mostly business. He added discussing the wedding to his to-do list. He didn't want a long engagement, and he hoped she didn't either, but they hadn't discussed it since he'd asked her to marry him. Talking was long overdue. He would give her the moon if she asked. All he wanted was for her to be his wife.

She came and sat with him in the living room.

"Are you planning on sitting here all day looking at that laptop, or would you be interested in taking a ride with me into town to get a few things for dinner?"

"Depends on what's on the menu for tonight?" Mark teased. He loved everything she made and she knew it.

"Baked mac & cheese."

He closed the laptop and put it on the coffee table. "You know what I like."

Bailey came into the room to join them. "I'm not interrupting anything, am I?"

Mark smiled at her. She was pale from the surgery, but she had a positive attitude about beating the disease. He was sure Hannah's endless encouragement and tender loving care contributed to that. From what the doctors said, once she was healed enough, she would need to return back to Rhode Island to start chemotherapy. Bailey was far from out of the woods and he would do everything in his power to make her as comfortable as he could, while loving Hannah and caring for her as she needed him desperately at this trying time as well.

"Plenty of room for you." Mark replied and scooted over, sliding Hannah closer to him.

Once she was sitting, she grabbed the remote control and flipped on the television. "There's supposed to be a college playoff game today I don't want to miss. It's supposed to start right after the local news. You guys want to watch it with me?"

Mark shot Hannah a look. "Sure, sounds great."

Bailey flipped the channels until she came upon the news anchor. He'd just finished a story about a local barn burning due to a lightning strike. *I don't watch the news. I have enough doses of reality as it is. I don't need to watch them feed me whatever made-up bullshit they decide I deserve.*

The anchor went on to the next story. This one caught his attention as well as the ladies in the room. He wanted to snatch the remote from Bailey and change the channel but that would be too obvious.

"The US Navy has uncovered a local terrorist cell here in Georgia. Thanks to their continuous efforts and bravery this cell was removed before any attacks could be made on American citizens. Although the Navy wouldn't provide the names of these heroes, we here in Georgia thank you. No details where the terrorists had been hiding out, or what their plans were, but we were able to obtain photos of the two men who were killed during the raid."

Mark saw both men's photos appear on the TV. *Fuck. Who leaked that shit? Their ass is mine if I find out.*

Hannah let out a high pitched screech then leaped off the couch and ran out of the room toward their bedroom. Mark started to get up but Bailey's words halted him.

"It really happened to her. She wasn't dreaming. Oh my God. Poor Hannah. We have to help her." Bailey reached out and grabbed Mark's arm desperately.

"What happen Bailey. Tell me so I know what we need to do to help her."

Bailey's hand was shaking as she moved to sit closer to Mark. She told him exactly what Hannah had told her. Mark thought he would be sick. As Bailey was explaining what Hannah had told her he knew exactly what the fucking assholes had used the Ketamine for.

They'd drugged Hannah so their movements wouldn't be noticed. That also explained why she had looked so tired when he'd first arrived but now her energy level was almost equal to his.

"Did she say that he ra . . . raped her?" Mark's voice never shook, but it did this time. This was the woman he loved more than his life, and what they had done to her physically hurt his heart as nothing in his life ever had.

"She blacked out or can't remember it, but from what she said he was doing that she could remember, I would say yes. No man would stop when he was that close to—"

Mark had heard enough. He needed to be with Hannah. Right now he wished he hadn't blown a hole in the back of his head because he wished he was alive so he could look him in the eyes and tell him exactly why he was going to fucking die. *And it wouldn't be such a quick and painless death either.*

When he entered the bedroom, Hannah was lying down on her stomach crying. She needed so much more than he could give her. She'd been hurt, violated in the most disgusting way and he could try to comfort her, but he knew she would need to speak to someone who could help her through this in a way he couldn't. *Damn, I hate not being able to make this go away. This is something where all I can do is love you and listen.*

Slowly as not to startle her, he laid down beside her and stroked her back. "I'm here, sweetheart. No one is going to ever hurt you again. I'll never let them."

She didn't look up at him, keeping her face buried in the pillow as she spoke. "Mark. It wasn't a dream. He really—"

"I know. I know. I'm sorry. I wish I could take it all away. But I can't. He's gone and he will never hurt you again."

"I don't understand. How come I couldn't stop him? How come I couldn't remember?" Hannah sobbed.

"Ketamine put you in a drugged state that you slept through. Somehow you were awake enough to remember, but not be able to do anything about it. It put you in a dream state."

He could feel the tension within her yet there was no way no matter how he tried, could he truly understand what she was going through. Mark had seen so much cruelty and violence over the years, but this one was affecting him physically in a way he's never experienced. He needed to remind himself that what he was feeling was nothing compared to what Hannah was. At some point he was going to need to deal with and process what happened himself, but this was not the time or place for that. All it would accomplish today was causing more pain to the woman he loved and he wasn't about to do that.

"I'm trying to remember, but it's like slow motion pictures. I can't tell what is real and what isn't. The more I try the more confused I get."

Don't ask her questions. Just listen and be supportive. Pushing her can break her.

"I know my love. We will get someone who can help you through this. You're not going to have to go through this alone. You have me and Bailey and there are people who are trained to help you sort this out."

"I don't want to talk to anyone, Mark. This is too embarrassing. I can't—"

"Hannah. Do you think I'm weak?"

She shook her head.

"I need help processing this. Let's find the right person who can help us both." He knew he'd never be able to share things within him that he should, but he would do anything for Hannah. If that meant meeting with someone once a week to talk about feelings, he would. He'd never be able to say what was truly in his heart, not to anyone except for Hannah.

She nodded in agreement. "I know. It's going to take time but I need to know what really happened. Otherwise I think it will haunt me forever. I don't want him to have any power over me, to hinder my life in any way. I refuse to let him take my future from me."

God, you're such a strong woman. What happened to you was horrendous. I hate to share you, but you have so much to offer this world. There are so many women out there that need to hear your voice, your message. And I'll be by your side all the way.

He wanted to hold her tight so she would feel safe. If only his love could heal her pain. No matter what it took, he would be there, and give up anything to ensure she was okay. Hannah had somehow become his whole life, his whole world. Nothing mattered to him if she wasn't okay.

"I love you Hannah." Mark whispered. He felt the tension ease and she relaxed slightly against him.

"Mark, do you know why? Why me?"

Because they are evil and wanted to hurt you. "I don't think that had been their first intention. I think the guy that hurt you did that on his own."

"So the others, what happened to them?"

"Both men were killed that day."

Hannah sat up, her cheeks still tear streaked as she said, "I mean the others."

"There were two here."

She shook her head in confusion. He knew something wasn't right. She closed her eyes as though trying to focus.

"In my dream I didn't see Jason, my tenant. There were only strangers. That's why I thought it was a dream. They spoke in a language I didn't understand, and I didn't know any of them."

Them? Shit. "Hannah, I hate to ask you to do this, but can you tell me who was in your dream? Do you know what they look like?"

She nodded. "The man with the scar. He's the one that—"

Mark nodded. "And you said there were others with him? And you're sure none of them were the tenant?"

"Yes, three others that I had seen."

Fuck. We need this information, and my love, you're the

only one who can give it to us. God I hate asking you to do this. But I need this to protect you.

"I could describe them for you. I know what they look like. Every detail is burned into my memory. I had wanted it out of my mind, but if it means I can help you catch those bastards, I'm glad it's still there."

My sweet brave girl. You never cease to amaze me. Here I am worried if you're strong enough to be the wife of someone like me, and I'm blown away; your strength is greater than many men I've served with.

"I can take you with me to a place where they will help you identify them."

"Yes. I want to help. It's not like what you do, but if I can help in this small way, I want to." Her voice was so adamant and strong.

And that led right into what he knew he needed to talk to her about. After what he'd just learned, he knew he could never leave her again. A deployment overseas could leave her unprotected for months. He'd never risk that.

"Hannah, I wanted to talk to you about that. I have my re-enlistment papers. I've decided not to sign them."

"No, you can't do that." Her voice rose.

He didn't understand her resistance to this news. If anything he'd thought she'd be elated about the decision. It was one he'd never had imagined making until Hannah came into his life. "I don't want to leave you. How can I protect you if I'm not here?"

Hannah reached her hand out and touched his

check. "I love you, Mark Collins, and that love cannot be broken. Not through distance or time. But what I have learned through this entire ordeal is that what you do is desperately needed. I need you, this country needs you, and this world needs you to sign those papers and find those bastards before they can hurt more people."

He looked into her eyes and saw love and respect in them. But after what had happened to her before he had arrived, how could he ever consider leaving her alone again? "Who is going to take care of you while I'm gone?"

Hannah laughed, "I will. What I've also come to realize is I'm much more resilient than I'd given myself credit for. Heck, I might even go back to college and get that degree I started years ago. I didn't think I had it in me to finish it any longer. It's like I had stopped dreaming when my father had become ill. With you in my life, the future is all I think about now. I have three more years but I really would like to finish it. If that's okay with you, that is."

College? Why not? You're brilliant and I want the entire world to know it. "I say follow your heart and I'll support you in anything you decide to do."

"Ditto."

"And what have you learned about taking care of yourself?" *I hope it was to trust no one.*

"To ask questions, lots of them. Knowledge is powerful."

She was so darn cute as she said it he almost laughed,

but he knew she was serious. And more importantly, she was right.

Pulling her into his arms, Mark said, "Knowledge is power, but do you know what is more powerful?"

She shook her head.

"Love. And you, my sweet Hannah, have all the power in the world, because I love you with all my heart."

The tears started streaming down her cheeks again, but his time he knew it wasn't pain and hurt. It was the same reason he had to fight back his tears. They had found the most precious thing in this world, soul mates. He would stay in the Navy—he had even more to fight for now. Mark knew from this day forward, Hannah would always be first in his life. This was something he promised for them both.

THE END

Other books by Jeannette Winters

Betting on You Series:

Book 1: The Billionaire's Secret (FREE!)

Book 2: The Billionaire's Masquerade

Book 3: The Billionaire's Longshot

Book 4: The Billionaire's Jackpot

Book 5: All Bets Off

Barrington Billionaire Series:

Book 1: One White Lie

Book 2: Table for Two

Book 3: You and Me Make Three

Book 4: Virgin for the Fourth Time (pre-order January 2017)

Book 5: His for Five Nights (2017)

Book 6: After Six (2017)

Southern Desires Series:

Book 1: Southern Spice

Book 2: Southern Exposure

Book 3: Southern Delight (Coming 2016)

Book 4: Southern Regions (Coming 2016)

The Billionaire's Secret

Billionaire Jon Vinchi is a man with one passion: work. His friends decide to shake him up by entering him as a prize at a charity event.

Accountant Lizette Burke is dressed to the nines and covering for her boss at a charity event. She's hoping to land a donor for the struggling non-profit agency that employs her.

She never expected to win a date with a billionaire.

He never thought one night could turn his life upside down.

One lie stands between them and their happily ever after. Too bad it's a big one!

Available now!